PRODU
SUPERHERO

Dan Luca is an expert coach, trainer and motivational speaker, specializing in productivity and work–life balance for entrepreneurs and everyone who strives for a better way of life. He helps people create a lifestyle that balances family, health, hobbies, spirituality and business, so they can live their best life possible. He has created two online programmes—the 5 A.M. Productivity Coaching for entrepreneurs and the 5 A.M. Online Club—for more than 1,000 early risers. Dan publishes strategies and systems that he has tested on thousands of his own coaching clients. Due to this extensive hands-on experience, he can vouch for his methods without blinking an eye.

The author is based in Romania. He has written the bestselling *The 5 A.M. Revolution: Why High Achievers Wake Up Early and How You Can Do It Too.*

PRODUCTIVITY SUPERHERO

Become The Most **Organized** and **Disciplined** Person You Know

DAN LUCA

RUPA

Published by
Rupa Publications India Pvt. Ltd 2019
7/16, Ansari Road, Daryaganj
New Delhi 110002

Sales centres:
Allahabad Bengaluru Chennai
Hyderabad Jaipur Kathmandu
Kolkata Mumbai

ISBN: 978-93-5333-330-0

First impression 2019

10 9 8 7 6 5 4 3 2 1

Printed by Nutech Print Services, Faridabad

Contents

The Acceleration

The High Speed

The Finish

The Extras: 5 Super Powers to be Used Daily

Introduction:
The Road to Freedom
through Discipline

*Self-discipline is a form of freedom. Freedom from laziness
and lethargy, freedom from expectations and demands of
others, freedom from weakness and fear—and doubt.*

—H.A. DORFMAN

I'm one of those people who love discipline, although I'll
confess I wasn't like this from the beginning.

Think about it, why would anyone love discipline? At
first at least, it seems like a limitation, a self-imposed
constraint...

However, if you take a closer look, those who are
disciplined are the ones who are truly free, while those
who seek to be free, no matter the cost, are the ones who

are conditioned and restrained.

I quite agree with what Steve Pavlina states, 'Self-discipline is the ability to get yourself to take action regardless of your emotional state.'

Taking action is the fundamental characteristic of remarkable people.

These successful people also have a few other traits in common:

- They deliver what they've promised…every time!
- They finish what they had started!
- They become better day after day because they study and practise.
- They have daily productive rituals and routines.

If you closely examine each trait, every one of them is screaming out—'discipline'. None of them would be possible in the absence of discipline!

Moreover, *each successful person knows that, if you don't control yourself, your circumstances will!*

For instance,

- You're not disciplined enough to pay your taxes on time, you pay the fine for being late.
- You're not disciplined enough to improve your English, you're not promoted to a managerial position.

- You're not disciplined enough to take your car to the service station and investigate the yellow light on the dashboard, one day your car will stop running and fixing it will cost you more time and money.
- You're not disciplined enough to save 10 per cent each month, you end up living without savings and in fear of the next day and so on and so forth.

The late Stephen Covey said, 'The undisciplined are slaves to moods, appetites and passions.'

Long-term indiscipline will cause you to lack abilities that could significantly enhance the quality of your life, for example, learning a foreign language, using text-editing software, studying parenting skills, etc.

Discipline also means taking action whilst thinking of the long-term consequences and not just how you feel about those over a shorter term. This means sacrificing a temporary pleasure for a significant long-term benefit.

Concretely, this shift in your perspective will produce the following changes in your unproductive behaviour:

- You'll continue to work on a project or idea even after the initial enthusiasm has worn off.
- You'll go to the gym even if you only want to sit on the couch and watch TV all day.
- You'll wake up earlier in the morning and work

with yourself for yourself.
- You'll say 'No' when tempted to give up on your diet.
- You'll check your social media only a few times each day (instead of innumerable times).

Discipline was also one of my weakest traits in the past. I missed many opportunities because I didn't have the necessary discipline.

However, I persevered, and I'm thrilled to tell you that today when I am writing this book, I woke up at 5 a.m., exercised, had breakfast and wrote in my journal.

It, most certainly, would have been more pleasant to lie a little longer on my comfortable bed. However, I made the decision that this 'pleasure' should subordinate itself to a higher one that has to do with my purpose in life.

I think discipline is that staircase anyone can climb when they've decided to escape their prison of mediocrity.

However, the good news and the bad news, at the same time, is that there's no middle ground... You either go up and start living a remarkable life, or you go down and sink deeper and deeper into your disappointments and frustrations.

And, for all of the reasons mentioned above, it's essential that you study and practise discipline!

It's probably the best thing you can do for yourself and your children!

Become the most disciplined person you know and inspire others as well!

Honestly, look at what changes discipline can bring about in your life, and what freedom—'I do what I want to, when I want to'—can get you. Draw your own conclusions and act accordingly.

I wish you become a life-long friend of discipline!

Who am I?

My name is Dan Luca and I am going to guide you through this potentially life-changing journey.

I am an entrepreneur, a productivity expert, a work-life balance coach and a super-dad. For as long as I can remember, I've tried to get the most out of my life, my time and my efforts. I went to great lengths—over a period of more than eighteen years—to achieve the level of energy, clarity and confidence that I enjoy today. I'll share my story, but before that, let me tell you this:

First of all, congratulations for mustering the courage to take the first step in altering things towards a more fulfilling life and for investing the time, energy and money to make it happen.

Secondly, I'll make sure that your journey through this course is gentle but steady, as well as show you all the pieces of the puzzle and the ways to implement them so that everything fits nicely together in the end.

Thirdly, all the things that are in this course are science-based, client-tested and time-proven, so that you will get all the advantages of our research, but without the hassle of testing them. Thousands of my clients are proofs that once you experience this change, you won't ever consider going back.

At each stage of the course, you will get all the necessary tools, templates and resources so that you can fully implement every bit of the information.

What drives me?

For as long as I can remember, I have enjoyed helping people fulfil their potential and not leave all the goodness inside themselves to go to waste. In high school, I was the go-to person for little personal dramas. I always had a kind word and a strategy for my teenage friends. So, you could say that I was already a natural coach back then.

At the same time, I was passionate about flows, processes and all kinds of improvements that brought about greater efficiency. It was natural that I would go on and do a business management course at the university.

Back then, way before knowing what I wanted to do with life, I made a promise to myself: if the management part would become my work, the people-development part would remain a hobby.

For about ten years, the deal that I had struck with myself worked out pretty well, and I explored a variety of positions—from being a Senior Buyer at a tech company to being a Financial Auditor at a Big Four Auditing Company, to being a Project Manager at a Training Company while getting involved in various interesting endeavours.

During that period, I witnessed and lived first-hand the eighteen-hour working days, a seven-days-a-week work schedule, and worked for months on end without rest and recovery even for a single day. So, I know very well what excess looks like. I know very well how it feels to lose all your friends due to an extremely tough workload. I know how it feels to wake up in the middle of the night simply because the figures don't balance on the spreadsheet.

This was one of the most important triggers that led me into the productivity field but without the excesses and the imbalances. I knew great things could be achieved without sacrificing health, relationships or selling one's soul.

After some extensive soul searching, I realized that personal productivity could bring together my two lifetime passions—personal development and systems improvement.

As Mark Twain once said, 'The two most important

days in your life are the day you are born and the day you figure out why.'

So, every day, I cherish the moment when I realized what my life is about.

Let's begin! See you at the starting line!

How to Get the Most
Out of This Book

After working with several thousands of clients, I am now able to clearly identify the patterns that ignite Superhero Productivity in people, as well as those that block any chance of great results in the least amount of time.

As a consequence of my years in the Productivity trenches, I have structured the book to follow these principles:

1. Bite-sized information for a daily intake that is not overwhelming, but easy to digest and implement right away.
2. A thirty-day approach that gives you enough time to implement and test ideas and see the changes happening in your own life.

3. World-class strategies, tools and exercises that are science-based, time-proven and client-tested, so you don't have to sort out what's working from what's not.

4. The optimum mix of structure, discipline and motivation over the course of 4+ weeks:

   a. Monday to Friday for strategies and tools for greater productivity

   b. Saturday for a recap of the main ideas and an evaluation form to help you get a clear picture of the progress you have made over the last seven days

   c. Sunday for an inspirational story, not to give you extra work, but to lift your mood and keep you connected to the journey

Remember!

My advice to you is to synchronize the structure of the book with the days in a week as soon as possible.

For instance, read and implement Day 1 on a Monday, Day 6 on a Saturday, Day 7 on a Sunday and so on. Read one lesson every day and do the recommended work so you build your Superhero Structure while being highly motivated and disciplined.

Let's begin!

THE PREPARATION

Day 1

Who Are Your Allies?

Discipline is the refining fire by
which talent becomes ability.
—ROY L. SMITH

Today is the first day of the thirty days dedicated to getting organized and increasing self-discipline.

I firmly believe that *the lack of organization and discipline represents the greatest obstacle to personal fulfillment.* I will explain why I believe this to be true later in the book. But first of all, I believe a definition of discipline is necessary to establish a frame of reference.

I find myself best represented by the definition Steve Pavlina gave for discipline. He said, 'Self-discipline is the ability to get yourself to take action regardless of your emotional state.'

And, if I were to follow up with what 'discipline' is to me, I would say *it is the ability to focus your available resources at the right time to achieve the desired result.*

Discipline is not that relevant if someone is not able to organize and prioritize activities.

As it turns out, smoking one pack of cigarettes a day is also a form of discipline and dedication.

To be disciplined can also mean eating the entire contents of your fridge after 8 p.m. It can also mean watching your favourite series daily...or complaining every day about how unlucky you are and how everyone's out to get you.

Obviously, this is not the sort of discipline I'm referring to.

I'm referring to the discipline that helps you evolve little by little every day.

- I'm talking about the discipline to read between ten to twenty pages daily.
- I'm talking about the discipline to exercise for at least twenty minutes.
- I'm referring to the discipline to say 'Please!' and 'Thank you!' after every human interaction.

Discipline, like many other traits, is a two-faced coin—one lifts you up and the other brings you down. Which one would you choose?

Since you could very well use a knife to cut a loaf of bread or kill a man…it becomes a matter of choice.

So, to answer the question—*What benefits do organization and discipline bring about?*—I will give you the reasons why you'll most likely want to avoid being disorganized and undisciplined.

- When you're not organized, *you don't have clarity* and this means perpetual stress and constant procrastination.

- When you're not disciplined, *it's nearly impossible to achieve long-term success* because this type of success requires the self-discipline to act out your plans regardless of the emotional state you're in.

- When you're not organized, *you have every chance of missing out on valuable details and pieces of information,* and this, in turn, will quickly result in failures and disappointments.

- When you're not disciplined and organized, *you'll fail to respect your deadlines* and this will bring about more frustration and stress; moreover, your partners, bosses and co-workers will lose faith in you and your promises.

- When you're not organized, *you're paid much less*

than those who are effective at their jobs. If it takes you two hours to do something that your co-worker gets done in just an hour, this means you're paid half of what your co-worker gets.

- When you're not organized, *you work overtime to finish your tasks,* you get home late and your loved ones are not happy about it.

Today's to-do list! (The best time to do it is NOW!)

1. Find your own definition of 'discipline'. You can complete the following phrase with three to five examples.
   'I feel I'm disciplined when...'
   'I feel I'm disciplined when...'
   'I feel I'm disciplined when...'

2. Find your own definition of 'organization'. As before, you can complete the following phrase with three to five examples.
   'I feel I'm organized when...'
   'I feel I'm organized when...'
   'I feel I'm organized when...'

Day 2

Hercules: Your Discipline Muscle

We must all suffer from one of two pains: the pain of discipline or the pain of regret. The difference is discipline weighs ounces while regret weighs tons.

—JIM ROHN

In the previous lesson, we talked about what 'discipline' and 'organization' are and what they aren't. This introduction was necessary so that you could begin forming your own opinion.

Any idea or theory that you hear remains in the 'what if' category until it's internalized by the one who hears it.

Your personal reasons will allow you to train your

disciplinary skills because, in many ways, discipline is similar to a muscle. The better trained this muscle is, the greater the challenge it can overcome.

Of course, if at this time your discipline 'muscle' is not that strong, we will focus on training it for the next twenty-eight days until you'll be able to rely on it completely.

Similar to any training programme, we first need to assess the starting point.

You'll find a few questions to think about below when you are assessing your starting point:

1. Do you wake up at the same time every day, even on weekends?
2. Do you make your bed in the morning?
3. Are you overweight?
4. Are you an addict (coffee, cigarettes, sugar, alcohol, etc.)?
5. Is your inbox empty (no unsorted or unread emails)?
6. Is your desk organized?
7. Is your house clean and organized?
8. When you make a promise to someone, in what percentage is it kept?
9. When you make a promise to yourself, in what percentage is it kept?
10. Can you fast for twenty-four hours?

11. How often do you exercise?
12. How many hours of focused work do you have in a regular day?
13. Do you have clear, written goals alongside a plan of action?
14. For how many hours do you watch TV each day? Could you not watch TV at all for thirty days?
15. How many hours do you spend on social media sites?
16. Are you in debt?
17. When was the last time you implemented a new (positive) habit?
18. When did you last give up on a negative habit?
19. Lastly, what's your perceived level of discipline— on a scale of 1 (min) to 10 (max)?

Now, after you have gathered some information regarding the aspects of your life where you lack discipline (or you don't), in the next few days we'll begin working with the perceptions, tools and motivations that will help you strengthen your discipline muscle.

TODAY's to-do list! (The best time to do it is NOW!)

1. Answer the fifteen questions.
2. Find at least five other areas where you believe a higher level of discipline could help you improve the

quality of your life (business, health, parenting, life partner, hobbies, etc.).

Day 3

Kryptonite: The Limiting Beliefs

*Begin challenging your own assumptions. Your assumptions
are your windows on the world. Scrub them off every once in
a while, or the light won't come in.*
—ALAN ALDA

In the previous lesson, we tested your discipline 'muscle'
to determine how effort-ready it is.

Today we'll be talking about how most people
sabotage themselves and don't even give themselves a
chance of becoming disciplined. This happens mostly
because they tend to have negative associations with what
discipline represents.

*At its core, ancient Greeks used the word 'discipline'
and it refers to the instructions given to disciples so that*

they may learn a skill or perform an action. It also refers to a certain code of conduct.

And yes, it can be perceived as a manner of following what those who are higher in rank tell you to do.

But let's do a small imagination exercise...

Let's replace that external stranger (master) with your own inner master!

Let's replace that external someone that wishes the best for us with our internal master that seeks our highest well-being!

Let's replace external constraint with internal dedication!

It looks a bit different, doesn't it?

A suited metaphor for this conversion is as follows: *'A diamond is a piece of coal that was exposed to an extraordinary amount of pressure.'* (Read extraordinary discipline.)

Then, if the practice of discipline brings about so many benefits, why is it so difficult for us to become friends with 'it'?

To answer this question, we need to analyse the *limiting beliefs regarding discipline that create this 'difficult relationship'.*

I don't know which belief resonates with you in

particular, but I will approach them one by one and 'dismantle' all…

1. **Discipline is a limitation on freedom!**
   False!

   'Self-discipline is a form of freedom. Freedom from laziness and lethargy, freedom from expectations and demands of others, freedom from weakness and fear—and doubt. Self-discipline allows a pitcher to feel his individuality, his inner strength, his talent. He is master of, rather than a slave to, his thoughts and emotions.'– H.A. Dorfman

2. **If I'm disciplined, I'm no longer spontaneous!**
   False!

   When you're disciplined, you can be spontaneous by choice and not because you're forced to! The undisciplined live with the sense that they're free to do what they want when they want.

   I believe they're free to adapt and react to what others are doing! Being disciplined when you need to 'build' is different from being creative when you need to solve problems.

   Without being able to make a decision or if you're lacking the discipline to build, what is left is a lifetime of fires that need to be put out and an endless stream of problems that need to be solved which will ultimately hold you back. Decide for yourself what path you'll choose.

3. **I've had a few successes; I can take a break.**
False!

Discipline is like a muscle. If not exercised, it atrophies and loses its effects. Each interruption warrants an exercise in willpower to resume productive and disciplined habits.

Avoid, as much as you can, the trap of 'just this time'. Each exception not only atrophies your discipline but it also weakens your self-esteem because you know you were weak and gave in (even if it was just that one time!).

However, when you don't give in, you strengthen your self-esteem and the certainty that you're in control of your own life!

4. **I want to be disciplined, but those around me get in my way!**
False!

Being disciplined is, first and foremost, a personal decision that you make. And, just like any promise that you make to yourself, you can either keep it or break it. It's possible to find yourself in a challenging environment where freedom (read 'chaos') reigns peacefully.

It's simple! You have a decision to make; you either control the environment or are controlled by it! As soon as it becomes obvious to you that you don't want to be controlled, you'll make the necessary adjustments to act in a disciplined and ordered manner.

5. I can't be disciplined because I lack willpower!
False!

Discipline is especially a structured and clear way of thinking. External discipline starts with internal discipline. Discipline is what decides 'what' things will get done and 'how'. Only afterwards will your 'willpower' spring into action as the muscle that executes what the disciplined mind has decided. This muscle doesn't act when it lacks the orders that it receives from the mind.

TODAY's to-do list! (The best time to do it is NOW!)

1. Carefully re-read the limiting beliefs regarding discipline and identify those you resonate with. Find your own arguments to refute your initial perception, the ones that will help you become more organized and disciplined.

2. Think about different areas in your life where you lack your desired level of discipline. Identify the story you

tell yourself to 'justify' this lack of discipline. Is this story real? Find evidence that it is false by looking back at your past experiences and look at other people who have overcome similar difficulties.

It is false as long as you find instances in the past where you or someone else found ways to get past that issue.

The North Star: The Higher Purpose

Nothing splendid has ever been achieved except by those who dared believe that something inside them was superior to circumstance.

—BRUCE BARTON

In the previous lesson, we talked about how perceptions can be major obstacles when it comes to implementing the habits of being organized and disciplined.

Today we'll talk about how all of these obstacles can be overcome when you have a good enough reason to do so!

Yesterday we had discussed the paradigm shift from external constraint to internal dedication. We had also touched upon the opportunity to connect with your inner master (your authentic self) and overcome the temporary shortcomings brought upon by applying discipline.

Jim Rohn said it very well, '*We must all suffer from one of two pains: the pain of discipline or the pain of regret. The difference is discipline weighs ounces while regret weighs tons.*'

However, if you wish to suffer the pain of discipline with a smile on your face, it's absolutely essential to clarify your final goal, destination or reward.

So, let's do a short exercise through which we can clarify 'why being disciplined is worth it.' We will be working with our four intelligences: body, mind, emotions and soul.

For your body:

- How do you see yourself in 20 years?
- What level of energy would you like to have?
- How do you perceive yourself healthwise?

Okay, now ask yourself the following question:

If you keep doing what you're doing right now...what are your chances of fulfilling the 'vision' that you have regarding your body?

For your mind:

- What level of productivity would you like to have twenty years from now?
- What level of mental clarity would you like to experience two decades from now?
- How disciplined and organized do you wish to be?

Okay, now ask yourself:

If you keep doing what you're doing right now...what are your chances of fulfilling the 'vision' that you have regarding your mind?

For your emotions:

- How much quality time would you like to have with your spouse and children twenty years from now?
- How much quality time would you like to have with your friends?
- What is the level of self-confidence you wish to have two decades from now?

Okay, now ask yourself:

If you keep doing what you're doing right now...what are your chances of fulfilling the 'vision' you have regarding your emotions?

For your soul:

- What career would you like to have twenty years from now that will fulfil your aspirations and fill you with satisfaction?
- How would you like to contribute to the improvement in the quality of life of your peers twenty years from now?
- What will be the level of gratitude and harmony you will experience?

Okay, now ask yourself:

If you keep doing what you're doing right now...what are your chances of fulfilling the 'vision' that you have regarding your soul?

You'll most likely notice that there is a distance—quite long for most people—between what you desire and where you're starting from.

And, with *a little bit of soul-searching, you'll remember that all of the significant progress you've made in your life has been the result of consistency and dedication. Or, in other words, discipline!*

Discipline goes hand in hand with productive habits and we'll study and practise them quite a bit during this course.

But, until then, I'll leave you to answer the questions regarding 'the best version of yourself,' which you would like to experience twenty years from now.

TODAY's to-do list! (The best time to do it is NOW!)

1. Sincerely answer the questions regarding the four intelligences.

   Reach to healthy conclusions and clarify the realistic outcomes that will come to pass twenty years from now if you don't change anything regarding what and how you're doing what you're doing right now.
2. Find the reasons why it's worth it to be disciplined— at least two reasons to begin with.

Let me give you a couple of personal examples:

I was inspired by my grandfather who, at ninety years of age, had the necessary health and energy to play with my two boys—his grandsons. This is why I exercise in the morning; I drink water as well as eat a healthy breakfast.

Another reason why it's worth it for me to be disciplined is that through everything I do, *I want to convince hundreds of thousands of people to wake up at least an hour earlier each morning and dedicate this time to themselves.* The potential of this single habit is immense. (My first book, *The 5AM Revolution: Why High Achievers Wake Up Early and How You Can Do It Too* reached #1 on Amazon worldwide in the Time Management category.)

One important reason is also that *I want to be an impeccable role model for my two boys.* I want to give them the opportunity to emulate the best version of their father and I don't want to burden them with my unresolved issues. This motivates me to work with myself on a daily basis to eliminate limiting beliefs, distorted perceptions, fears or any other constraints I might pass on to them consciously or subconsciously.

Day 5

Your Excuses and Other Fairy Tales

Don't be afraid to be extraordinary!

—TUT IRWIN

Hello!

In the previous lesson, we went on a journey through time so that you might have the opportunity to visualize the future that you desire. I hope you have started to see more clearly the difference that 'discipline' can have in your life.

Today, we'll move on and talk about *the stories we tell ourselves to keep us in place so as to avoid change and progress.* They're also the reason why we fail to accomplish our goals and lack discipline.

These are the most common eighteen stories we tell ourselves to avoid bruising our egos through failure.

Unfortunately, however, *these are the exact reasons why we fail to move forward to reach our full potential and why we don't inspire others to live their lives fully as well.*

I'm curious to see which ones you identify yourself with:

1. It's going to be hard

It certainly won't be easy...but is it important enough for you to invest the necessary time and energy?

2. It's risky

Every step forward requires a certain amount of uncertainty. Take smaller steps to diminish the risk but keep moving forward.

3. It's going to take a long time

It might take a while but you know what? Time will pass no matter what you do; whether you start doing what is right or not, time will pass either way!

4. It's going to create family drama

The only drama that already exists in your family is the

fact that you are not living up to your true potential. You're not allowing yourself to be all that you can be and you're also not allowing those closest to you to do the same.

5. I don't deserve more

Of course you do! And, if you analyse your past, even if you were using this excuse, you received much more in many ways. It's true, maybe you didn't receive as much as you could have, but at no moment in time did you experience the river of life drying up.

6. It's who I am

Wrong! It's who you are now and, with each passing second, you change little by little. Were you the same person a week ago? A month ago? Five years ago? Humans never stay the same, so stop clinging to this false perception.

7. I can't afford it

This is a very toxic belief that has its roots in the past. Your future will be the same as your past only if you want it to be that way. I would suggest a small but powerful adjustment for this limiting belief, 'I can't afford it...yet!' Ask yourself afterwards, 'What could I do to afford it?'

8. No one will help me

Of course, no one will help you if you don't ask for help! This belief, by itself, has the power to become a self-fulfilling prophecy: 'I have this belief', 'I don't ask for help' and 'what do you know?' 'No one helps me!' As soon as I hear this phrase, I immediately ask the person, 'How many people have you asked for help?' I think you can guess the answer I normally receive.

9. Things have never gone my way

'Never', 'always', 'every time'…these are negative generalizations and they are the greatest enemies of personal growth. Let me ask you this, 'Never?', 'Always?', 'Every time?' The answer will obviously be, 'Not really.' Change your perception to change your reality. Even Dyer said, 'When you change the way you look at things, the things you look at change!'

10. I'm not strong enough

This belief makes me smile. How did you conclude that you aren't strong enough? When was the last time you gave it your all and failed? Remember…your ego doesn't want to get bruised, but most of the times, your self-confidence will appreciate a victory even at the expense of a bruise you received when you stepped out of your comfort zone.

11. I'm not smart enough

You don't have to be! There are so many people out there who have already made it and who could teach you how to do it as well. No matter the challenge you face, there's certainly at least one other person who has faced the same challenge and has overcome it. Seek that person out and you'll find the solution without having to invent it yourself.

12. I'm too old

Do you mean to say you have a lot of experience? Does the task require physical effort you can't manage? Find a young man, place him under your wing, inspire him and let his enthusiasm do all the work.

13. I'm too young

This could have been a good excuse if the World Wide Web hadn't existed. Now, no matter how young you are, you can set your ideas in motion in simpler and faster ways than ever before. The internet offers equal opportunities to everyone.

14. It's overwhelming

To me, it sounds more like, 'I do a lot of unimportant tasks and I don't know how to prioritize.' Study productively, clarify your priorities, identify the tasks that generate the highest value and commission the rest.

15. I don't have enough energy

This is my favourite excuse I hear during my coaching sessions. It can be solved in three easy steps. Go to bed at 10 p.m. Wake up at 5 a.m. Use the time between 5 a.m. and 7 a.m. to take a walk, exercise, drink water and eat a healthy breakfast. I'll guarantee you'll have a surge of energy the entire day!

16. My family history is to blame

When I hear this excuse, I ask people, 'Do you want your children to say the same thing about you? That because of you they missed out on life?' Even if your family's past is not an easy thing to bear, switch gears. Take full responsibility and change things so that the legacy you leave behind for your children will be a healthy one.

17. I'm too busy

Often when I hear this excuse, I smile and ask, 'Busy

doing what?' Nine times out of ten answers I receive comprise superficial and highly emotional arguments that essentially translate to, 'I don't know how to be organized, and I lack discipline.' As you already know, by studying these two abilities, you increase the quality of your life.

18. I'm too scared

I'm going to let you in on a little secret: we're all afraid when we're doing something for the first time, but some of us choose to act despite our fears. The moment you face your fears is when you feel most alive because it's in those moments that you feel that you're evolving.

It's possible that your excuses are a combination of some of the eighteen mentioned above or you might even have a personalized version of the excuses that you tell yourself.

If that little voice in your head tells you: 'My excuse is unique; it's not amongst the 18. So, there's still no solution for it...,' I advise you to practise the following exercise, which comprises a few questions:

1. Is what I'm telling myself true? Is it *really* true?
2. Do I want to take full responsibility for everything that happens to me?
3. What will happen if I keep believing the story I tell myself?

4. What would my life look like if I stopped hiding behind excuses?
5. Can I find a rational reason to change?
6. What's the first step?

And, like any practice, it will become more and more effective if applied more and more often. Give yourself the chance to escape your excuses this way.

TODAY's to-do list! (The best time to do it is NOW!)

1. Carefully read the eighteen excuses and identify the three you use often. Starting from the arguments I gave you, find at least three other ways of looking at your excuse from the opposite angle (find ways to deconstruct your excuses rationally).
2. Practise the six-question series on three other excuses that are currently holding you back. They can be either a part of the eighteen excuses mentioned above or a part of those 'special and personal' excuses you haven't found in the list.

Day 6

Recharge and Prepare (Part I)

Be yourself, everyone else is already taken.
—OSCAR WILDE

The first week has come to an end!

And because it's a Saturday morning, *you'll find two things in this lesson: a weekly summary and an evaluation questionnaire regarding the progress you have registered.*

Read the main ideas and answer the questions to complete the first week.

Okay then, let's see what you've learned this week.

Day 1: What benefits do organization and discipline bring about?

Essential idea:

We've identified what beneficial discipline and what harmful (but disciplined) habits mean. In addition, you've found your own definitions for discipline and organization.

Day 2: How well-trained is your discipline muscle?

Essential idea:

You've answered the fifteen questions that will help you paint a clear picture regarding how well-trained your ability to be disciplined is at this time.

Day 3: Limiting beliefs regarding organization and discipline

Essential idea:

I have deconstructed the five harshest limiting beliefs regarding discipline. Find yours and eliminate them as soon as possible.

Day 4: The higher purpose that fuels discipline

Essential idea:

We went on a journey into the future to twenty years

from now, in which you painted a picture of what you would like your future to look like when it comes to your body, mind, emotions and soul. Of course, the essential resource required to reach the desired destination was... discipline.

Day 5: What would your life be like if you stopped using excuses?

I deconstructed the most frequent eighteen excuses people give themselves to avoid leaving their comfort zone and experiencing failure. In addition, I gave you a set of six questions that will help you break apart any other 'special excuse' you might have.

Okay, now let's see how well you navigated your first week:

1. On how many days (out of five) did you practise the exercise for each lesson? (0-5) >
2. How many minutes, on an average, did it take you to complete the daily exercise? >
3. What topic from these first five days have you found most relevant or revealing and why? >
4. How happy are you with the progress you've made? (1–not happy at all; 10–very happy) What changes would have made your score 1–2 points higher? >

33

5. How dedicated are you to continue to improve your level of organization and discipline? (1–not at all; 10–very dedicated). >

If You Believe It, You Will See It!

Not a lot of people know this, but due to complications Stallone's mother suffered during labor, the lower left side of his face is paralysed, including parts of his tongue, lip and chin. This incident at birth is the cause of his trademark snarling look and his slurred manner of speaking.

For the first five years of his life, Sylvester Stallone bounced from one foster home to another, while his parents fought and squabbled endlessly in a bad marriage.

Although he was eventually reunited with them, his troubled past and his oddly paralysed face made him an outcast among his classmates. He often received suspensions for his frequent fights, poor grades and behaviour problems.

His adult life was just as difficult. Hard times and a lack of income resulted in the actor getting evicted from his apartment. As a result, he was forced to live on the streets for close to three weeks.

Eventually, he came across a casting call for an adult film. Out of desperation, he attended the casting call. For a two-day filming period, the actor received $200.

According to Stallone, *'It was either do that movie or rob someone, because I was at the end—the very end—of my rope.'*

He made the decision to try his hand at writing various screenplays. However, he found himself broke once again. In an act of desperation, he waited outside a local liquor store asking people if they would buy his dog, Butkus, his closest and best friend. In the end, someone bought his dog for roughly $40.[1] Stallone was devastated that his life had come to that point.

Two weeks later, the historic fight between Muhammad Ali and journeyman boxer Chuck Wepner inspired Stallone, as Wepner hung around for 15 rounds

---

[1] https://www.huffingtonpost.in/entry/see-sylvester-stallones-wistful-tribute-to-rocky-dog-and-pet-butkus_us_58de24b2e4b05eae031ee677, accessed on 30 November 2018.

and even managed to knock Ali to the ground in round 9.

That match gave him the inspiration to write the script for the famous movie, *Rocky*. He wrote the script in 20 hours! He tried to sell it, and got an offer of $125,000 for the script. But, *he had just one request*. He wanted to star in the movie. He himself wanted to play Rocky, but the studio declined his request. They wanted a real star such as Ryan O'Neal, Burt Reynolds or Robert Redford.

They said he 'looked funny and talked funny.' He left with his script. A few weeks later, the studio offered him $250,000 for the script. He refused. They then offered $350,000. He still refused. They wanted his movie, but not him. He said no. He had to be in that movie.

Finally the studio agreed, gave him $35,000 for the script and let him star in it!

The first thing he bought with the $35,000 was the The dog he had sold. Yes, Stallone loved his dog so much that he stood at the liquor store for three days waiting for the man he had sold his dog to. And on the third day, he saw the man coming with the dog.

Stallone explained why he had sold the dog and begged to have him back. The man refused. Stallone offered him $100. The man refused. He offered him $500. And the guy refused. Yes, he refused even $1000. And, believe it or not, Stallone had to pay $15,000 for the dog he had sold at $40 only! And he finally got his dog back!

The rest is history!

As you probably know, *Rocky* became a worldwide commercial success and Oscar winner. The film was nominated for ten academy awards in all, and went on to win academy awards for Best Picture, Best Director and Best Film Editing.

The sequel, *Rocky II,* was released a few years later, which also became a major success. The film series had grossed more than $1.25 billion at the worldwide box office.

Moral: Follow your instincts. Don't give up on your plans. Go all the way! Be your greatest fan!

THE START

Day 1

These Enemies Will
Destroy Your Work

*Order and simplification are the first steps toward the mastery
of a subject.*
—THOMAS MANN

Last week, we talked about what a life without excuses
would look like and we dismantled the most common
excuses.

Today, on this first day of the second week, we will
be actually rolling up our sleeves and effectively diving
into the topics of organization and discipline.

Throughout the first week, we analysed the general
framework, the motivations and significance you offer to

these two aspects of your life.

Consequently, today we'll be approaching things that could sabotage your organization and planning and ultimately, your productivity.

Let's begin with a very interesting piece of information.

Studies regarding work productivity have shown that a person works at a job, on an average, less than 49 per cent of the effective work hours. This diminished percentage is mostly influenced in a negative way by the often internal (created by yourself) or external (coworkers, bosses, suppliers, customers) interruptions.

And, if this unwanted situation is so largely spread out, it generates a few consequences: half of a person's potential is not reached, half the possible sales are not finalized, and half of the possible income is not earned!

An essential element of any productivity system—whether it's professional or personal—is the existence of a balance between effectiveness and efficiency.

Simply put, *effectiveness means doing things well and fast.* You're effective when you fulfil a certain task—important or not—in the most economical way possible.

Efficiency means doing the right things. You're efficient when you do the tasks you need to be doing to reach your goals.

The general belief is that if you're effective, you're also efficient—which is not always true. You can keep busy all day long talking on the phone, holding meetings, sending emails only to realize at the end of that day, week or month that you haven't done much at all.

It's good to keep in mind the following two ideas regarding effectiveness and efficiency:

1. If you do an unimportant task well, that task doesn't become important.
2. The fact that a task requires a lot of time does not make it more important.

It's useful to see these distinctions when you are deciding how you're going to invest your time so that your decisions will bring about better results in the long term. Moreover, you need to pay attention to these 'three perverse enemies of productivity':

1. Frequent interruptions

When an interruption occurs, your mind is sent wandering in another direction. The mind then wastes a lot of productive time to return to what it was doing before being interrupted, to re-enter the right state and to resume generating optimal results.

Your mind needs at least ten minutes to focus on a medium to high complexity task and at least ten minutes as well to change the context. So, every time you change context, you lose, on an average, between ten and twenty minutes.

2. Start and Stop

This 'enemy' is connected to those frequent interruptions, but it's also an effect of a lack of planning regarding the activity that you wish to finish.

For instance, I need to work with a co-worker for the common project of the two departments. I usually see my co-worker at his desk, and most times, he's open for conversation.

My assumption is that he'll be available anytime to work together for an hour on the project. Consequently, I don't talk to him to set up a date and time for our meeting. And when I seek him out to work together, I find out he's not available. Hence, I start and then I stop.

3. A succession of tasks unrelated to each other

For instance, I answer a co-worker's email, then I call a supplier, then I have a meeting with a department manager, I answer another email, I call a customer, I talk to my boss, etc.

This succession of tasks entails an enormous amount of time wasted to enter and exit the optimum state of performance. Moreover, it generates a high level of stress which, in turn, gives rise to the feeling of being overwhelmed.

TODAY's to-do list! (The best time to do it is NOW!)

1. Take five minutes and analyse your To-Do List for today. Do you need to shift your priorities to be both effective as well as efficient? How can you make sure you're going to meet both requirements?

2. Analyse your personal level of productivity. Count how many times you're interrupted daily by external factors, whether it's a co-worker, a phone call, an unread email, an impromptu meeting, etc.

3. Count how many times you interrupt yourself—in an unscheduled manner—from what you were doing. It could be remembering something you forgot to do, or maybe you find yourself suddenly hungry or thirsty, maybe you realize your eyes or your back is hurting.

Day 2

The Winning Edge

We are not what we know
but what we are willing to learn.
—MARY CATHERINE BATESON

In the previous lesson, we talked about the three enemies of productivity, and how you can become effective and efficient.

Now we'll be talking about *the simplest way of setting priorities so that we're not just effective at what we do but efficient as well.*

For this purpose, we'll be using the Priorities Pyramid model, which is very simple and clear. By applying its principles, you'll always be able to tell if what you're doing is the best thing you could be doing at that time.

The Priorities Pyramid Model has four levels and the following characteristics:

Level 1: Added value for your entire life (personal level)

Health and vitality—rest, exercise, relax, nutrition intake, breathe and stretch.

Harmonious relationships which include spending time with the most important people in your life.

Growth and development activities that help you achieve your mission in life.

On the other hand, it could be a combination of the three mentioned above—you watch a good movie with your children, you discuss plans with your spouse, you have dinner with a friend at a vegetarian restaurant, etc.

Level 2: High added value per hour (professional level)

The activities that have a high added value per time unit can be divided into two categories:

Time spent on preparation: Reading, planning, strategic thinking, networking, creating systems, prospecting

Time spent on performance: Sales, negotiations, coaching and sales writing

The two parts of this level can be seen as the training practice and the game or as the seed and the fruit.

Level 3: Low added value per hour (professional level)

The activities that have a low added value per time unit are mainly related to *maintenance*—administrative tasks, answering unimportant emails, moving papers, finishing reports, paying bills, etc.

Level 4: Zero or negative value per time unit (mostly personal level)

These activities not only add no value at all but they can also diminish your energy level through their counterproductive characteristic—worrying, gossiping, aimlessly surfing the internet, unhealthy eating, watching talk shows and broadcasts that stimulate conflict and discontent, traffic jams, etc.

For most people, activities in level 4 are done quite often, whereas those in level 1 are rarely done. For a few people, level 1 activities prevail followed by level 2, 3 and 4 activities which receive much less time.

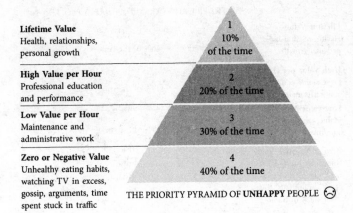

Lifetime Value Health, relationships, personal growth	1 10% of the time
High Value per Hour Professional education and performance	2 20% of the time
Low Value per Hour Maintenance and administrative work	3 30% of the time
Zero or Negative Value Unhealthy eating habits, watching TV in excess, gossip, arguments, time spent stuck in traffic	4 40% of the time

THE PRIORITY PYRAMID OF **UNHAPPY** PEOPLE ☹

No matter the situation you're in, it's important you realize that you can shift these ratios as long as they are significant enough for you to do so.

Shifting from a life where inferior levels prevail (3 and 4) to a life where superior levels dominate (1 and 2) requires discipline, ambition and significance.

This shift is not easy, but once you change your perspective, there's no turning back because you realize how vigorous life can be!

A life where activities in Level 1 and 2 prevail ensure a high level of significance and offers you the comfort of knowing you're living your life purposefully. Moreover, this is exactly how the pyramid for top performers looks like.

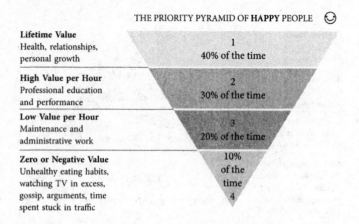

THE PRIORITY PYRAMID OF **HAPPY** PEOPLE ☺

Lifetime Value Health, relationships, personal growth	1 40% of the time
High Value per Hour Professional education and performance	2 30% of the time
Low Value per Hour Maintenance and administrative work	3 20% of the time
Zero or Negative Value Unhealthy eating habits, watching TV in excess, gossip, arguments, time spent stuck in traffic	10% of the time 4

Practically, the place you feel most fulfilled is at the crossroad of the first two levels (1 and 2) with your area of expertise—both professional and personal. I'm referring to that particular area where you can generate high quality results by putting in a small amount of effort because you've already achieved a certain level of excellence that allows you to do so naturally.

For instance, *in my case*, this crossroad occurs when I'm at my best physically, mentally, emotionally and spiritually, and only then I hold coaching sessions.

For a *painter*, it could be achieving the best creative state and then painting a masterpiece.

For a *leader*, it could be the moment when his vision becomes clear, and he enters his best state before conveying his vision and inspiring the people who put their faith in every word he says.

For a *salesperson*, it could be the time he allots to practice the best attitude, comprising of passion and contribution so that he can ultimately offer the best solution to every customer he encounters.

And so on...

So, you indeed control how you plan your day and how much attention you give to those aspects that generate the highest added value per hour or even for your entire life.

Consequently, take full responsibility of designing your own life by choosing to spend most of your time between the first and the fourth level activities!

TODAY's to-do list! (The best time to do it is NOW!)

1. **Look at your task list for today.** Next to each activity, place the number that corresponds to the level of that activity (1 through 4).
2. **Determine the load of the tasks you practise during your active hours** (from the time you wake up you wake up and until you go to bed).

For instance:

Active hours: 18

Total time spent on the third level: 3 hours

A percentage of 3/18 = 16.6 per cent

- For level 1: hours and minutes spent_____

       meaning a percentage of _____

- For level 2: hours and minutes spent_____ meaning a percentage of_____
- For level 3: hours and minutes spent_____ meaning a percentage of _____
- For level 4: hours and minutes spent_____ meaning a percentage of_____

3. **Identify the other tasks you are yet to complete** and determine their load for each level.

At the end of this week, sum up the time you've spent on each level and determine the shape of your pyramid and the weight each level has.

Day 3

5 Essential Mind Shifts

If your actions inspire others to dream more, learn more, do more and become more, you are a leader.
—JOHN QUINCY ADAMS

In the previous lesson, we explored a very simple manner in which you can clarify your priorities so that you might know, during each moment in time, if you're doing the right thing that will provide you long-term benefits.

Today, we will be discussing the newest paradigms that top performers have. What might have worked in the past might become the very obstacle towards reaching the next goal.

I want to ask you now if you've noticed some subtle

changes lately in the top performers you know...

You might have noticed them but not realized what those changes have been exactly or why they have been 'embraced' by these people.

Top performers have stopped applying the old paradigms and have started embracing new ones.

To be more specific:

1. **They've stopped being so preoccupied with time management; they've started being more interested in energy management. Why?**

    We all have the same 24 hours in a day that we try to split up and allocate, but not all of us have the same level of energy.

    You can plan to finish a task in 60 minutes, but if you don't have the right energy, you won't even finish it in 2 hours.

    This is why energy management has become the first step towards productivity!

2. **They've stopped looking at life like a marathon; they've started looking at it as a series of sprints. Why?**

    The optimal way of using your energy is through short but tight time slots followed by an equally tight recovery time slot.

POMODORO **CYCLE**

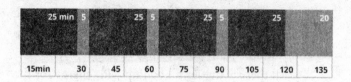

■ **WORK** ■ **BREAK**

In other words, optimal performance comes in the shape of an oscillatory wave.

- Up for an intense (but not long) period
- Down for the necessary recovery period

These intensity fluctuations maximize long-term productivity.

3. **They've stopped considering breaks a waste of time; they've started viewing them as productive time. Why?**

This is because breaks are like the pit stops in a Formula 1 race. You fill up the tank of your car, change the tires and clean the helmet visor so that you can race at the maximum speed safely.

During your work breaks, you can take care of your body (water intake, stretching, nourishment, relaxation), emotions (relaxing conversations with co-workers, talking to a family member on the phone, analysing your internal state) or soul (expressing gratitude, nourishing your values, realizing the contribution your work brings to others, etc.).

All these activities fill you up with energy for the next super-productive time slot!

4. **They've diminished the importance of rewards; they've increased the importance of significance. Why?**

People indeed have material needs but more than that, they need to know that their work is significant and in accordance with their values and beliefs.

For instance, someone who values the environment and the well-being of animals might feel extremely demotivated if they're asked to work in a company that tests their products on animals.

5. **They've diminished the importance of positive thinking; they've increased the importance of total immersion. Why?**

This is because when you're 100 per cent involved in a project, it's not just your mind that's in it that helps you keep your hopes up. You're physically, mentally, soulfully and emotionally invested in that project. You find yourself in everything you create and the result ends up representing you almost completely.

I've given you these perspectives so that you may start to have a more nuanced understanding of what a success strategy looks like for those who have become top performers in today's world.

These new principles are indeed different from those used ten to twenty years ago, and I'm sure you want to be on the front lines of productivity, organization and discipline.

TODAY's to-do list! (The best time to do it is NOW!)

1. Carefully reread the five perspectives. Identify the ones where you need to shift from the old paradigm to the new one.

2. Find your own reasons for wanting to adopt these new paradigms and identify one or two concrete ways through which you can apply them, starting today.

3. Closely observe the productive people you know and identify the things they do differently than most people. What are those things?

Day 4

Are You Your Greatest Saboteur?

Self-sabotage is when we say we want something and then go about making sure it doesn't happen.
—ALYCE CORNYN-SELBY

In the previous lesson, we talked about the new paradigms that top performers live by. Have you appropriated them yourself? Are you willing to start applying them from today?

Today we'll be dealing with sabotage, especially the one that we create for ourselves.

If you took a little time to analyse yourself, you might have noticed that the challenges generated by your external reality are far smaller than those created by your internal one.

There's even a famous saying in this regard, *'Get out of your own way!'*

There is a lot of truth to this statement.

The lesson we can derive from this is simple. Get out of your own way, understand how you're sabotaging yourself and do those primary tasks that help you become organized, disciplined and productive.

Let me show you how.

To make things as clear as possible, I'll start from *the premise that each of us is a system comprising four elements: body, mind, emotions and soul.*

This system, as a whole, functions at its best when all of its four parts receive attention and energy.

When this doesn't happen, friction appears between these elements, each one claiming its rightful place.

For instance, if I work for hours on end at my desk without taking a break, my body will send me a signal through a stitch, a numb leg, etc. It's another way of saying, 'Hello, I'm in need of your attention!' *Essentially this is the reason behind self-sabotage and procrastination!*

The cost of an action requires attention and energy, which should be devoted to another element. In the above-mentioned example, your mind consumes the energy necessary for your body. And the latter element is not very keen on being left behind. So it fights back, or, in other words, it creates certain internal blockages.

The necessary solution is handy, but it's not a corrective, rather an anticipatory one!

Prevention is the best solution to maintaining harmony between the four intelligences: body, mind, emotions and soul.

Each of these intelligences has a distinct characteristic and each can be measured to find out if every element is receiving enough energy and attention.

Your body needs energy.

Your mind needs clarity.

Your emotions need confidence and harmony.

Your soul needs significance.

Why? Allow me to get into the details.

1st situation:

You have clarity, you are confident and clearly know 'why' you want to do something, but *you don't have an ounce of energy to get out of bed.* So, you're getting nowhere.

2nd situation:

You have the energy and the confidence, you know 'why', *but you lack clarity and direction.* You're like a fly flying like crazy through a room, hitting its head on every wall, trying to get out. You're active but you're not getting anywhere.

3rd situation:

You have the energy, the direction and you know 'why' *but you don't believe that you can do it; you don't have faith you can achieve the desired results.* Fear of failure paralyses you. So, you're at a standstill.

4th situation:

You have the energy, the direction, the confidence *but you lack a strong 'why'.* You start a project, work on it for a short while and give up because something more interesting catches your attention. You start off well, but you give up because your interest in that activity begins to fade.

The four situations illustrate what happens when you achieve sub-standard results. One or more of your four vital elements is unavailable. Therefore, instead of having an extra resource, you end up having an extra internal conflict.

The following quote by Eldridge Cleaver illustrates this idea perfectly:

'*You either have to be part of the solution, or you're going to be part of the problem.*'

What can you do then?

The solution is getting these parts to work together for the unique benefits derived from the result.

Thus, they won't perceive the situation as the victory

of one part to the detriment of another.

Since I understood this holistic perspective, I could no longer set a goal that didn't take into account all these parts of myself.

Let me give you an example of how a holistic goal regarding weight loss looks like to me (or to the clients I work with).

Usually, people 'go on a diet'; then, they go to a wedding, and then, it is 'goodbye diet!' Or, they start exercising; then, they have to go on a business trip, and then, it is 'bye-bye exercise!' And so on...

Their pattern is 'putting all of their eggs into one basket' or 'betting everything on a single card', and 99 per cent of the times, they lose this bet with themselves.

Now, I'm going to describe *how the holistic goal of losing weight looks like by taking into account all of the four parts of ourselves:*

For your body:

- Balanced diet
- Exercise (fitness, aerobics, spinning, etc.)
- Daily 30-minute walks
- Dancing
- Rest
- Relaxation
- Massage

For your mind:

- Affirmations regarding your optimal weight
- Visualizing your desired silhouette
- Printing out photos of people who look fit and inspire you to get in shape
- Modelling the strategy of those who have managed to lose weight

For your emotions:

- Journaling when your emotional eating pattern is triggered
- Speaking to inspirational people who exude confidence and are successful
- Emotional Freedom Technique (EFT) to diminish your cravings
- Understanding the deep emotional wounds that you try to heal by consuming food

For your soul:

- A daily practice of the Hawaiian forgiveness therapy called Ho'oponopono
- Connecting to your authentic self
- Why do I really want to lose weight? Connecting to your personal values

And so on...

I think you've already got the picture about what I'm actually trying to say.

There's a huge difference between relying on the leg of a single table and the legs of a table (the number of items mentioned above).

If that single leg is destroyed, the entire table falls apart. But if your building stands on 18 pillars, your chances of succeeding are extremely high even if you lose half of them.

So, don't neglect any of the four intelligences because they will riot and sabotage your success!

The best thing you can do for yourself is to nourish these intelligences every day from the moment you wake up! This is why waking up at 5 a.m. makes so much sense! You are proactive and nurture the key elements of the system that will support you through any activity you wish to do.

You'll notice, with astonishment, that your internal resistance has diminished—almost disappeared—because there are no more internal struggles between the internal parts who are fighting for the resources of attention and energy!

Therefore, start practising those productive habits and allot the first two hours of the day to yourself for nourishing your 'best friends': your body, mind, emotions and soul.

TODAY's to-do list! (The best time to do it is NOW!)

1. Remember the three moments in your past when you fell prey to self-sabotage. Which of the four intelligences were not included in the goal you were looking to accomplish?

2. Identify a present situation where you feel you're self-sabotaging. Analyse your goal and find a benefit for a particular intelligence and an activity that will support the achievement of your goal.

Day 5

The Black Holes that Suck the Energy Out of You

If I want to be great I have to win the victory over myself...
self-discipline.

—HARRY S. TRUMAN

In the previous lesson, we talked about how to stop sabotaging ourselves and how to take into account the system's need for harmony.

Today, we'll be continuing down the same path with things to avoid or eliminate before becoming truly 'organized' and 'productive'.

Yesterday, we spoke of energy, clarity, self-confidence and significance.

Well, *there's a sure-fire way to ensure that you have none of the resources mentioned above. This way involves spreading yourself too thin or, in other words, to start a hundred things and not finish even one of them.*

This is a guaranteed recipe for failure!

You want to know what's interesting though? On a short-term basis, you might be under the illusion that if you multi-task (in other words, work on many things at the same time), you're being productive!

False!

You can truly believe that because you're constantly moving and consider yourself on the right path but that's not the case.

Even Mozart once said, '*The shortest way to do many things is to do only one thing at a time.*'

Remember: You need to be both—effective and efficient—to experience maximum productivity!

So, today we'll be talking about how we deal with the things we start but never finish, things that follow us around and consume an enormous amount of energy without offering us anything in return but anxiety, frustration and a feeling of being overwhelmed.

We'll be talking about the **Open** (and unclosed... obviously) **Loops Audit**.

'I'll deal with this later', 'It's not the best time right now', 'I don't have the energy' or other similar affirmations actually signal that we are in the grasp of an unending loop where we begin one thing without, however, managing to finish it.

I am not sure who it was, but the person who said the following was quite right. *'A person's level of harmony is opposite to the number of open loops that are left hanging...'*

Even though I knew this to be true in my case, transforming this idea into action happened over several months of agony, even for me, during which time I continued to 'carry on my back' all of these loops until the following thing happened.

I decided to make a list of all my open loops!

My financial 'background' (financial auditor, to be more specific) tempted me and so, I named my list: The open loops audit.

Afterwards, through self-practice and coaching sessions with my clients, I refined a model that does its intended job and helps you, specifically, to:

Identify + Estimate + Decide + Act with regard to anything you have ever started but have never finished.

In fact, this model can actually reduce the amount of time you need to close these loops that weigh you down by 50 per cent, 70 per cent or even 80 per cent.

So, to be more specific, the following is the manner in which you apply this model:

1. **You make a list of all of the things you have started but have never finished**

   The email you should have sent to that customer whose payment you never received, negotiating the terms of the contract with your supplier, paying your life insurance, keeping track of your income and expenses, etc.

2. **Make a list of all the things that bother you**

   Even if you're not the one to blame for these things (a damaged door handle, a worn-out toothbrush, the used heels of your shoes that need fixing, the missing button from you coat, etc.

3. **Estimate the percentage of completion for each of these unfinished loops**

   Estimate the percentage from 0–99 per cent.

4. **Estimate the time you'll need to close the loop at 100 per cent**

5. **Take one of the following decisions:**

   a) **Take responsibility for finishing the task**

   Open your planner and write down a day that would be most suitable for you to close the loop and how much time it will take, then CLOSE IT!

   b) **Delegate the responsibility of finishing the task to somebody else—either for free or pay for it**

   This proxy could be an employee, a member of the family, a friend or a service supplier, etc.

c) **Decide never to finish the task and take responsibility for all of the consequences of your decision**

Notice the keywords I used: 'Take responsibility for ALL of the consequences.'

d) **Decide to close the loop temporarily until you obtain more resources or information**

BUT establish, right then and there, when you're going to evaluate this loop again and take one of the aforementioned decisions—a, b, c or d.

Let me direct your attention to a few examples,

Example no. 1:

Context: You're hesitating to ask your service supplier for better contractual conditions

Percentage of completion – 70 per cent

The percentage is so high because you started negotiating 2 weeks ago and you agreed on the general outline of the contract, but there are still certain aspects that don't match your intentions.

Time needed for completion:

- Call your lawyer and schedule a meeting – 5 minutes
- Consult your lawyer and modify the contract – 1 hour
- Call your supplier and schedule a meeting – 5 minutes
- Meet with your supplier and renegotiate the contract – 1 hour

Total time required: 2 hours and 10 minutes

Example no. 2:

Context: You can't find the necessary time to fix the leaking water faucet in the bathroom.

Percentage of completion – 25 per cent

Until now, you've asked around about some good plumbers and you already have the phone numbers of two people.

Time needed for completion:

- Call the first plumber and request a price estimate for the repairs – 5 minutes
- Call the second plumber and also request a bid – 5 minutes
- Call the chosen plumber and schedule a date and time for the repairs – 2 minutes
- The actual repairs – 30 minutes

Total time required: 42 minutes

It's true that sometimes complications may arise along the way. However, the odds of this decrease dramatically when you have a plan to stick to.

From my own experience, I can tell you that without this type of mini plan, where the key word is 'clarity', these kinds of activities can take 2, 5 or even 10 times longer and they tend to consume a lot of your energy or, in other words, they tend to destroy a lot of your energy.

You must never think like this...

'Oh well! Big deal! The water faucet in the bathroom is not leaking anymore.' Yes, but the effects of closing the loops will accumulate because, when you carry 10, 20, or 50 open loops around with you, your life resembles that of a professional firefighter with you putting out fires all day long.

I don't know about you, but to me, this doesn't sound like a good life.

To have a real shot at gaining your energy back, you need to stop and take time out for yourself!

And, once you've done that, things will start running more smoothly!

TODAY's to-do list! (The best time to do it is NOW!)

1. Identify your open loops. This process might last a couple of days but start your list right now.
2. Estimate their percentage of completion and the time required to finish them.
3. Make one of the four decisions regarding each loop.
4. Act!

Day 6

Recharge and Prepare (Part II)

*What lies behind us and what lies before us are tiny matters
compared to what lies within us.*

—RALPH WALDO EMERSON

The second week has come to an end!

As usual, you'll find this week's summary and the
evaluation questionnaire that will measure your recorded
progress below.

Okay, let's see what you've learned this week.

Day 8: The three enemies of organization and discipline

Essential idea:

We unearthed the combined power that effectiveness

and efficiency have. Then, we shone a light on the three greatest enemies of productivity: 'Frequent interruptions', 'Start and Stop' and 'Unrelated activities'.

Day 9: Criteria for establishing daily priorities

Essential idea:

The simplest way to set priorities objectively is by using the Priorities Pyramid. This principle of establishing a hierarchy uses the 4-level model regarding the importance of invested time in certain activities.

Day 10: The 5 new paradigms of top performers

Essential idea:

Top performers have changed the rules of the game to adapt to the conditions present in today's world. You've learned the five most important perspective shifts they've made to stay on top.

Day 11: How not to sabotage your organization and discipline

Essential idea:

Self-sabotage is what happens when four of your intelligences don't receive their fair 'share'. Your body needs energy, your mind needs clarity, your emotions need confidence and harmony, and your soul needs significance. When you feed all four intelligences, you lead a balanced and harmonious life.

Day 12: The open loops audit

Essential idea: 'A person's level of harmony is inversely proportionate to the number of open loops that are left hanging.' I've shown you the simple way in which you can start closing the loops you still have open.

Okay, now *let's see how well you fared after your second week*:

1. On how many days (out of 5), did you practice the exercise for each lesson? (0-5) >
2. How many minutes, on an average, did it take you to complete the daily exercise? >
3. What topic from this second week have you found most relevant or revealing? Why? >
4. How happy are you with the progress you've made? (1 – not happy at all; 10 – very happy) What was required to increase your score by 1–2 points? >
5. How dedicated are you to continue to improve your level of organization and discipline? (1 – not at all; 10 – very dedicated) >

Day 7

Don't Listen to the Know-it-all Stupid People

There was this elderly man who had a profitable little business selling hot dogs on a busy street corner in a big city. He wasn't particularly well educated, but he sold great hot dogs and his customers loved him.

During the early morning rush hour, he'd wheel his mobile hot dog stand to position it near the exit of the central railway station in town. A year ago, he'd added a bacon and egg roll to his range and sold scores of them to this breakfast crowd every day. At lunchtime, he'd move his stand to a popular park where he had queues of regulars.

In the afternoon, he'd be back at the station entrance

and then later, mostly at night, he knew a great spot near a nightclub where patrons rushed him off his feet. He had even installed special lighting and a flashing neon sign. Even people driving by would stop.

He'd worked hard for years and done well enough to put his only son through a university who later became a management consultant with a large firm.

One day, his son warned him that a recession was on the way. The old man asked his son what this meant. As an educated man, his son gave a very detailed explanation of how the recession would severely affect every person in the community, particularly small business owners like his father. There would be widespread unemployment; people would not be able to afford to spend money as they did now.

He painted a gloomy picture of the future and warned his father that it would be wise to cut back on his expenses and 'tighten his belt' financially and prepare for the worst. The old man didn't know much about the economy or interest rates, but he trusted his son. After all, he was an educated man. Recession mentality kicked in.

The old man began to cut back on the quantity of sausages and bread rolls he bought. He didn't want to get caught with stale rolls as business began to drop off. But it was hard to judge, and some days, he actually ran out of sausages and rolls earlier than he normally would.

So he went home early and spent more time worrying about this recession that was coming.

Soon he knew that what his son had said was right. He noticed that his takings were indeed falling. This depressed him more and so he got out of bed later each day. After all, why get to the station so early when obviously more people would be eating at home rather than spending money on breakfast in the city? He decided that his bacon and egg rolls were too expensive for most people now. After all, they were twice the price of a hot dog, so he cut them from his menu and his sales continued to plummet.

Wow, his son was right, this recession was hitting hard!

He decided to save more money and not replace the batteries that powered his neon sign and lights at night. Now, because he was in the dark, fewer people bought from him and soon he decided that it wasn't even worth his time setting up at night. Eventually, he decided to sell off his equipment and his trolley.

He was in luck though because the woman who bought his trolley didn't seem to know how bad business was, or how severe the recession was going to be. He managed to unload the trolley for more than he thought he would get. Now, day after day he stayed at home, depressed, and occasionally his son would visit him and they would discuss how bad the recession was, and how lucky the old man had been to have an educated son who had warned him in advance about this terrible recession.

Moral: Our thoughts create our reality!

THE ACCELERATION

Day 1

Impeccable without Obsessive Compulsive Disorder

'Order is the shape upon which beauty depends.'
—PEARL BUCK

Last week, we talked about the open loops audit and how you can increase your energy level by resolving these unfinished activities.

Today, we'll be talking about something elementary but very important! We'll be discussing order as an integrated part of organization and discipline.

We all remember what adults told us when we were kids: 'Be more organized!', 'Clean your desk!' or 'Pick up your clothes and stop leaving them hanging around!'

What's interesting is that we naturally have a higher or lower tolerance towards disorder or 'chaos'.

Some people are bothered even by the crooked position of a book in their library whilst others couldn't be bothered even if their whole library was on the floor in disarray.

So, it's important to take this aspect into account and not pursue a dramatic overnight change from disorder to impeccable order.

But if order is already a part of your life, then congratulations, you're in the right spot!

Still, why is order so important? For two reasons:

1. **Our external environment influences our internal one:** This means that external disarray generates an internal one, and no, I don't think this particular state is called 'creativity'; it's called disorder!

2. **Our internal environment influences our external one:** Sloppy thinking generates and maintains external disarray and we end up where we started, only worse, because time and energy were spent without any outcome.

Consequently, *without order, there can be no organization, discipline or productivity!*

I'm NOT suggesting that you start moving mountains.

What I propose instead, is that you allot two five-minute time slots each day for the specific purpose of maintaining order on your desk and computer.

Two 5-minute periods each day!

Start practising them and over the next couple of days, you'll notice:

- An increase in mental clarity
- An improved psychic state
- An ease in solving problems
- A diminished feeling of fatigue

Are these improvements worth ten minutes each day? Absolutely!

One important thing to do!

Set up these two order periods in the morning and do them when it's time!

How to apply these order periods:

1. After use, archive every document to its designated spot (folder, document tray etc.).
2. Twice a day, clean your desk of papers, pens and any other unnecessary elements that cause disorder.

3. On your desk, 90 per cent of the time, there should only be your computer, phone, planner and a pen. Ten per cent of the time is dedicated to those moments when you work with documents, books, manuals or other printed works.

Watch out for your counter-productive internal dialogue:

'I don't have time to clean my desk now; I'll do it later.' 'It'll take me an hour to organize my desk; I'd better do it tomorrow.'

TODAY's to-do list! (The best time to do it is NOW!)

1. Schedule the two order periods for your desk.
2. Place a post-it somewhere on your desk where it's easy to see with the text: 'Archive documents after use, keep desk clean and organized. Before leaving the office, make sure that your desk is in an impeccable state for the next day.'
3. Adopt the following belief: 'I'm ordered and this helps me be organized and disciplined!'

Day 2

The Italian Way of Being Productive

I never could have done what I have done,
without the habits of punctuality, order, and diligence,
without the determination to concentrate
myself on one object at a time.

—CHARLES DICKENS

In the previous lesson, we talked about order as a way of working and thinking.

Today, we're going to take another step in this direction and we'll be talking about *one of the most powerful methods I know when it comes to boosting productivity.*

It may seem simple, too simple to work even, but I

assure you it's 'almost' perfect in many ways.

I invite you to give this practice a serious chance, then reap the rewards and share the 'secret' with those you care for.

This habit made a huge difference in how I work and generate results. The difference was so significant that I can't compare this technique with any other method of increasing productivity. It's the first and most important rule I apply, on a daily basis. I'll briefly tell you how to improve you productivity the Italian way.

These are the main steps on *how to practise the Pomodoro Technique:*

1. Set a kitchen timer or your phone alarm to ring in 25 minutes.
2. During this time, work non-stop, focusing completely on what you're doing.
3. After these 25 minutes, take a 5-minute break to refresh.
4. After four Pomodoro sessions, take a longer 15–20-minute break.
5. Repeat this process as many times as you can throughout the day.

Be mindful of:

*   The level of significance each activity on your list has

- How you estimate your time during the planning phase
- External interruptions
- Internal interruptions

24 reasons why the Pomodoro technique doubles your productivity

1. *You can't get started until you have a 'to-do' list* with the tasks you plan to do. So, you eliminate 'chaos' right from the start.
2. For this technique to work, *you need to establish your priorities and start working on your priority #1.*
3. *You know when to start and when to stop.* You estimate each task using Pomodoro units (3 x Pomodoro, ½ Pomodoro, etc.).
4. *You break your bigger activities into smaller, more actionable tasks.* In other words, you answer the question 'What's the next step?' Therefore, you eliminate procrastination because you have the necessary clarity and you know how much energy you have to invest in your next step.
5. *You work on a single task at a time.* Multi-tasking is thereby 'cured'.
6. *You group similar activities and act on them in the same time interval.* Your mind will be grateful to

you because you won't be forcing it to shift so many variables it has to work with; thus, saving a lot of mental energy.

7. *You more accurately estimate how long each task is going to be.* At first, you might not be so perfect, but the practice of estimating the time required to finish an activity will shortly become one of your abilities.

8. *You refine your planning process* and are able to determine more precisely the steps needed to reach your destination. Your thinking becomes much more practical since you're focusing on the next actionable step.

9. *It's easy to practice and it doesn't require hard-to-find elements.* Just a piece of paper with your to-do list, a pencil or crayon to cross each finished element off your list and a time-checking device: an alarm clock, phone alarm or kitchen timer (Pomodoro). If you're working on the computer, you can use Focus Booster (www.moosti.com).

10. *You don't mentally exhaust yourself* because you plan your recovery breaks before you get started.

11. *You take short breaks often*—after each 25-minute Pomodoro session—and after four sessions, you take a longer 20-minute break.

12. *During the break, you take care of your body.* You hydrate yourself, get up from the desk and do a bit

of stretching, have a light snack.

13. *During the break, you take care of your emotions.* You call a loved one, talk to a co-worker and check your internal emotional state.

14. *You relax your mind regarding anything external and focus only on what you have to do.* You log out of your email, set your phone on silent, ask your co-workers not to interrupt you if they see you focused on what you're doing.

15. *You increase your capacity to focus on just one thing at a time.* Top performers finish one task at a time with excellent results and don't do 10 things simultaneously with mediocre results.

16. *You resolve your internal interruptions* (those that come from inside of you). I mean, the moment you get an idea regarding a project or another activity, you write it on a handy piece of paper—two to five words to remember your idea—but you keep doing what you are doing until you finish the Pomodoro session you've started.

17. *Getting closer to a deadline (even one you set) stimulates your internal resources to focus.* Therefore, you synergistically work with every resource you've got.

18. *You increase your motivation and maintain it at a constant level until the end of the day.* When you see

how productive you become, you won't want to stop. I'm serious!

19. You become aware of a false issue these days. The fact that *there are a lot of less urgent matters that need to be tended to and that cannot wait for one or two Pomodoro sessions,* meaning 30–60 minutes.

20. *You increase the quality of your results because you give everything you've got during that Pomodoro session.* In that moment, there's nothing else for you to do other than what you're doing until the twenty-five minutes are up.

21. *You improve your discipline of not letting yourself get distracted.* This will help you make clear distinctions between the various activities you're doing. You stop mixing work with relaxation. You work intensely and focus for twenty-five minutes and then you relax for five minutes. And, after 2 hours, you take a 20-minute break.

22. *Pomodoro helps you develop a more effective study and work process.* You begin assimilating a higher quantity of information when you're studying because you maintain the optimal state for this activity longer. Your mind detaches itself from the process at one point if it doesn't clearly know 'how long' it will be to reach the destination. Predetermined periods are beneficial because they keep your mind fired up.

23. *At the end of the day, you know exactly what you did.* You know how many complete Pomodoro sessions you've had and you know what you've worked on during each session and the result you had.

24. *Pomodoro helps you become very productive without having to sacrifice your physical health or emotionally burden yourself.* Alternating between periods of intense work and periods of relaxation for your body and emotions makes a significant difference because you help your entire system maintain its balance. Consequently, you maintain a high level of energy and you end up working eight to ten hours super-intensely and generating qualitative results that will be hard to believe for those who work with you.

TODAY's to-do list! (The best time to do it is NOW!)

1. Read the twenty-four reasons why the Pomodoro technique will boost your productivity.

2. Set out to practise at least two Pomodoro sessions today (and in the following days). This means you would be implementing, in the next few days, two 25-minute sessions where you're working non-stop and focusing on just one task at a time.

Day 3

Genius Depends On This

It's not that I'm so smart, it's just that
I stay with problems longer.
—ALBERT EINSTEIN

In the previous lesson, we talked about the miraculous Pomodoro technique—the one that can do wonders if it's applied!

Today, I would like to talk to you about *five principles that will allow you the opportunity to increase the quality of your results as a consequence of increasing your power of concentration.*

Apply these principles and I guarantee that you'll experience highly productive and satisfying days from now onwards!

1. Clarify what's important (See the Priority Pyramid)

You have no chance of being truly productive if you're working on low-ranked tasks. Eliminate your fear of failure and dive into those tasks that have the potential of generating the most relevant results.

Performers take on the responsibility of learning from every feedback they receive as a result of their activities, even if they too have their own share of failures. However, they never negotiate their number one priority.

2. Clearly establish your top five priorities for the day

Let me tell you a secret. Start with the first priority, then move on to the second and so on. The more priorities you are able to finish from the top five, the better you'll feel at the end of the day.

On the other hand, if you start doing the fifth, then the fourth, etc., but never get to do the first, the things you've managed to achieve will end up amounting to diddly-squat.

Your number one task will place you among the performers if you finish it or it will hold you down in a mediocre state if you don't. So, choose wisely!

3. Abolish multitasking!

This is our modern disease and unfortunately, it's not showing any signs of going away. Instead, it's only spreading! How do you see yourself if you continue to work in the same rhythm? How many things can you juggle at the same time?

Any performer will tell you that they work on just one thing at a time and dedicate their mind, body and soul to it. They stay focused until they finish their number one priority, then they move on to the second. It's the only long-term viable solution!

4. Close your social media!

I hope you didn't feel any pangs throughout your body. Just kidding, but just like any addiction, when you interrupt the stimulus, you'll 'physically' miss it. This is a sign that something is wrong.

If you don't check your social media every five minutes, congratulations! However, if you have a compulsion to stay up-to-date with everything (even if it's something completely irrelevant to what's important to you), look objectively at this behaviour and notice what you'll gain and lose in the long term.

5. Take breaks and reward yourself!

Let's talk about Pomodoro again. As I said yesterday, it's a genius technique in more ways than one. It allows you the opportunity to take short and frequent breaks.

Each break invigorates you and gives you the chance to recharge for the next sprint. It's unbelievable, but you can actually work between eight and ten hours a day, productively, without exhausting yourself. Don't take my word for it, try it out yourself!

These principles are essential if you want to be organized and disciplined, and I would like to add three interesting and very useful perspectives.

Be glad when you have nothing to do!

When was the last time you had nothing to do? I'm asking this to motivate you to increase your productivity so that you can experience more of these moments. The way most people operate is like a recipe for failure.

They put so many things on their plate that they can't finish them all in one day, and then, they get frustrated. I call this process 'carried over frustration' as it is carried over day after day.

We're addicted to wasting time

Emailing, using Facebook, texting, surfing the internet, etc., are all beginning to turn into serious addictions.

We think it is okay because everybody is doing it. But if tomorrow everyone started stealing, would you do it too? Be smarter than that and take the necessary measures that will allow you to focus better and realistically increase the quality of your life.

When you're focused, you're unstoppable!

You won't believe it until you do it! You can reach the performance of finishing in a day what used to take you a week.

However, you need to ask yourself a very uncomfortable question: 'Am I wasting time instead of doing what's important?' If the answer is 'yes', then step out of your trance and start acting. Trust me; it's for your own good!

TODAY's to-do list! (The best time to do it is NOW!)

1. Reread the five principles and identify those you're still not applying. For each of them, find one thing you can do to start implementing that principle (for instance, organize your schedule using Pomodoro sessions, and, during your break, get up from your desk and drink a glass of water.

2. Mentally separate your productive peers from the unproductive ones. Promise yourself to spend as little time as possible with those who waste time

and interact (and let yourself be inspired) as often as possible with highly productive people who have high professional standards.

Day 4

Nobody Should Ever Do This!

Discipline is the bridge between goals and accomplishment.
—JIM ROHN

In the previous lesson, we talked about the fundamental principles of concentration. It's such a rare ability that those who practice it are either geniuses or top performers.

In this lesson, we'll be discussing the challenges your memory has to overcome when it comes to organization.

I will present you with a very simple system through which you can make sure you won't forget anything; furthermore, you'll have everything neatly organized and set-up.

Sounds too good to be true, right? Don't answer this question yet. Just wait and see.

One of my very good friends once shared with me a quote that I'll remember all of my life. He said, *'Our mind's main purpose is to be creative and not to store information. The busier it is with remembering stuff, the less available resources it has to create.'*

Seems obvious, doesn't it? Then why do we burden our minds with a great deal of mostly useless information and hamper our efforts to be creative to our fullest potential?

To draw a parallel with what we talked about in the lesson regarding the Priority Pyramid, I would say the current situation looks like this:

'Remember to pay *that* bill, to call George, to order an ink cartridge, etc.' All of these are third-level activities that don't bring about any added value per time unit.

Instead, I could be asking myself, 'How do I find out what my customers want?', 'How can I improve this product?', or 'How can I reduce the costs of transport?', etc.

Notice the necessary difference in thinking quality?

So, I encourage you to use this simple system to organize your thoughts and information, and it will free up a lot of creative energy that you can then spend on the first and second level activities from the Priorities Pyramid.

Collecting ideas in writing, then sorting, prioritizing and planning them

How to practice:

1. Buy a post-it cube (500–1,000 square post-its, preferably in different colours).
2. Buy a tray or improvise with a box you can use to store these written post-its.
3. Allow yourself two intervals throughout the day (after lunch and before leaving office) to sort and prioritize the ideas.
4. Plan the specific date and time for executing that task using your planner or calendar.

I really like this quote: '*A brilliant idea usually visits you once. You'd better take advantage of it.*'

Be mindful of:

- The thought that 'you'll remember that later', so you don't need to write it down
- Writing a single idea on a post-it
- Periodically revising that box or tray
- Executing that specific task at the scheduled moment

TODAY's to-do list! (The best time to do it is NOW!)

1. Buy or search your desk for a paper cube with post-it notes.
2. Buy or improvise a tray or a box where you can place your ideas written on post-its. A single idea per post-it!
3. Schedule the interval when you'll revise what's in the tray and decide how you're going to handle them. After you've scheduled the ideas in your planner, it's best if you throw out the post-its and leave the box empty.

Day 5

Who Is Your #1 Fan?

'Snowflakes are one of nature's most fragile things, but just look at what they can do when they stick together.
—TOM WROOT

In the previous lesson, we talked about how you shouldn't rely on memories and how you can implement a very simple system to capture and implement your ideas.

In this lesson, we'll be discussing *two complementary principles: focusing your work on similar activities and scheduling your strategic and creative thinking interval during the most productive time slot of your day.*

Organization and discipline have the final purpose of increasing productivity and this means better results, which will be achieved faster whilst consuming less resources.

We've already approached the enemies of productivity, so now we'll talk about two 'friendly' resources when it comes to the time and energy you invest.

The first resource has to do with grouping and finishing similar tasks during the same time interval.

How to do it:

1. Collect all of your incoming ideas using the tray or box described yesterday.
2. Group similar activities in the same time slot—phone calls, emails, meetings, sending offers, searching the web for information, etc.
3. Execute these blocks of similar activities during productive Pomodoro sessions.

Be mindful of:

1. *The situations where the information needs to be sent quickly* (for instance, after finishing a call with a customer, he asked that you send him a certain piece of information to make the purchase). However, you must not use this situation as an excuse to lose your focus.

   Monotony and saturation. If your productivity

begins to suffer, you can shift between tasks and time segments to add a bit of variety.

It's true you'll lose a little time while entering the new segment, but you would have already suffered from a decreased productivity level if you had continued with the initial task.

For instance, if you have scheduled three Pomodoro sessions to send out invoices, you can insert a 25-minute session after the second Pomodoro, in which you send offers to clients.

I think this practice is simple enough and further explanations are not necessary.

However, this principle becomes even stronger if you combine it with the following:

Allot the first 30 minutes to 2 hours of your workday as individual thinking time.

Brian Tracy said, '*Every minute you spend in planning saves 10 minutes in execution.*' In contrast, there's a saying I passionately hate: '*We're workers, NOT thinkers...*'

So, allot the first part of your work schedule for strategic and operational thinking. This time you're investing has the potential to generate so much clarity regarding what you have to do that it might surprise you when your day becomes as easy as a stroll in the park.

In a previous email, we talked about how not to sabotage your success, and one of the main causes of self-sabotage mentioned was the lack of clarity.

Eliminate this obstacle right from the start and you'll enjoy a super productive day.

How to practise it:

1. Keep your planner free during the first 30 minutes up to 2 hours out of your workday.
2. Use this time for strategic and creative thinking.
3. Aim to finish four highly productive Pomodoro sessions during these two hours and include the most important activities of the day.

Be mindful of:

- *The need to socialize with your co-workers first thing in the morning* (remember that some people are addicted to wasting time...)
- *The necessary time you need to prepare before you start working* (Is your desk in order? Do you have the necessary information? Is your water glass or tea cup nearby? And so on...)
- *The unproductive manner in which some people start their day with a meeting* for which they haven't had the time to prepare properly. The direct consequence is that the meeting lasts longer than necessary and diminishes your productivity.

TODAY's to-do list! (The best time to do it is NOW!)

1. Allot at least the first Pomodoro of the day towards strategic and creative thinking.
2. Group the similar activities you have to do today in a single block.
3. Work using Pomodoro sessions and you'll be surprised how much your productivity will increase in a few short days.

Day 6

Recharge and Prepare (Part III)

There is only one corner of the universe you can be certain of improving, and that's your own self.

—ALDOUS HUXLEY

This third week has come to a close!

I'm curious how you have evolved, what challenges you have faced and what 'A-ha!' moments you've had.

Okay, let's see what you've learned this week.

Day 15: Order as a way of working

Essential idea:

Order can be a treacherous and subtle saboteur. Your mind works clumsily when it has to sort out chaos. Give it an environment that is as ordered as possible and it will work more productively.

Day 16: When organization and discipline meet, Pomodoro is born

Essential idea:

The Pomodoro technique is the best kept secret of increasing productivity. In addition, this method alone can increase your productivity by two, three or even five times. You can't afford not to use this technique.

Day 17: The strategy of a genius—the ability to focus

Essential idea:

Increase your ability to focus by taking into account these five simple and easy to apply principles. Enjoy the times when you have nothing to do and avoid those people who waste time.

Day 18: Your memory is not reliable. Here's how not to depend on memory...

Essential idea:

Use this simple method using paper cubes to write your ideas so that no 'brilliant' idea gets away. Use your mind to create and not store information.

Day 19: How many 'golden' minutes do you allot daily?

Essential idea:

Collect your ideas, group them according to their common characteristics, and finish them during highly productive Pomodoro sessions. Moreover, don't let anyone take away the first 30–120 minutes of your productive workday. Think, create and plan for more effective and efficient days.

Okay, now *let's see how well you fared after your third week.*

1. On how many days (out of five) did you practise the exercise for each lesson? (0–5) >

2. How many minutes, on an average, did it take you to complete the daily exercise? >

3. What topic from this third week have you found most relevant or revealing? Why? >

4. How happy are you with the progress you've made? (1 – not happy at all; 10 – very happy) What was required to happen so that your score would have been 1–2 points higher? >

5. How dedicated are you to continue to improve your level of organization and discipline? (1 – not at all; 10 – very dedicated) >

Day 7

At What Age Will You Stop Learning?

On the day of college admissions, a young man was getting ready to continue his journey of accumulating even more knowledge, an adventure he began a long time ago, that seemed to have no end.

Lost in his own thoughts, his mind immersed in what was going to happen in the future, he barely noticed the old man he bumped into.

'I'm sorry, professor!' the young man said, feeling embarrassed.

'Oh, I'm not a professor,' the old man answered. 'I'm a new student, just like you.'

The young man was shocked to hear this. He asked, 'Well, how old are you?'

'Seventy-three,' he said with a playful glow in his eyes.

'And what will you be studying?' the young man went on to ask.

'Medicine. I've always wanted to become a doctor and now...,' the old man paused like he was trying to remember something that had happened a long time ago. '...Now I can finally pursue my dream!'

The young man was shocked by his answer.

'Excuse me, sir, but to become a doctor you need at least seven years of college. In seven years you will turn 80.'

The old man put his arm over the boy's shoulder, looked him in the eye and answered with a smile, 'God willing, I'll turn eighty, if I follow my dream or not. Time will pass either way...'

Moral: Age should never be a deciding factor in determining the things that you pursue. You can be happy going to medical school at eighty years of age and miserable in the same school at just twenty years of age. Regardless of the pursuit, if it answers 'yes' to the question 'will it make me feel more alive?' it should be high on you priorities.

THE HIGH SPEED

Day 1

How Not To Ruin
Your Work Relations

Drop the idea that you are Atlas carrying the world on your shoulders. The world would go on even without you. Don't take yourself so seriously.
—NORMAN VINCENT PEALE

Last week, we talked about how you can organize your ideas and execute them as a group to increase your effectiveness. We also discussed how allotting time for yourself in the morning can lead you to excellence, while not doing so can keep you in an 'okay-ish' zone.

Today, we'll be referring to a topic that's painful, especially for those who have to lead people, teams or companies. It is regarding delegation.

Unfortunately, many people believe they know what delegation is; however, that's not the case at all.

Delegation consists of a couple of principles, and if you don't apply them just right, the entire process will be a failure.

What I will be presenting below is a strategy used by a friend of mine who owns four businesses and works with more than fifteen people at the same time.

What's truly different about this strategy compared to other cases is that *people take responsibility, perform at an excellent level and are delighted by the process.*

To me 'to delegate' doesn't mean: 'Here's what you have to do…get on with it, do what you know, just deliver results!' And, you'll understand this after reading the ensuing information.

One more thing: *This strategy is presented from the perspective of the person who delegates, meaning from the manager to the employee.*

BUT…*even if certain tasks are already being delegated to you, the information below can be used to change how the delegation process works!*

The feeling you'll get will be something along the lines of: 'How have I been working in such a way for such a long time?'

Read, understand and then apply and you'll see how

different the results are!

There are two lists.

The first explains what you have to do when you delegate, and the second list explains what not to do when you delegate.

What to do when you delegate:

100 per cent responsibility for only one person—The person to whom you delegate something must know that he has 100 per cent responsibility for the result of the delegated task. It is not the responsibility of those he works with. As a result, apologies such as 'I didn't do that because John from marketing didn't give me the design in time' will not work.

Clarify the result and write it down—Yes, I know you know it; you find this in many management books, but I want to say it again just to be sure. Clarify with your employee what would be the concrete, visible result of the task. When you arrive at a clear understanding of that result, tell the person to write it down, and also write it down yourself.

Ask for a deadline—Yes, I said it right—ask, not assign! Ask the person when the task will be complete. Then ask: 'Why is it going to take you so much time?' Then, 'Can you do it faster?' Next, ask: 'How could you do it in half the time?' This way, you assure yourself that the deadline is right and at the same time, the other person is responsible because you didn't give him the deadline, he assumed responsibility for the deadline.

Write down the deadline—Take out your planner or your delegation template in front of the person and write it down. This way, you make the person more responsible because he knows that you also wrote down the deadline and now he's committed to it. If you are not present physically, and are talking on the phone, tell that person, 'Wait a second, because I want to write the deadline down.'

Ask about the consequences—Again, ask, don't tell! People are more open to respecting what they come up with on their own, instead of what other people tell them. Afterwards, ask the next question: 'Do you take 100 per cent responsibility for the deadline you gave me?' The obvious answer will be 'yes'. Then, ask: 'Now tell me what the consequence will be if you don't meet this deadline?' If he doesn't know, give him some options like: a 10 per cent salary cut, working overtime, and so on (even though I don't agree with employees working overtime).

Write down the consequences—The same thing you did for deadlines. When the person sees that you are writing down the consequences, it will increase his level of personal responsibility, knowing that he has agreed to the consequence.

Schedule the next appointment—Write down the date and time of your next meeting to discuss the result of the delegated task. Even if that meeting will be only five minutes long, it is really important for the successful completion of the delegated task. He or she will need to meet with you in person and see the planner or template where you wrote down the deadline and consequences.

I know it may seem like a long and a difficult process to apply, but trust me, it's not! In the beginning, it might take you longer, but once you learn the process, it will take you just as long as it does now. Only, the long-term results will be extraordinary!

No exceeded deadlines!

No hassle!

No wrong or misunderstood results!

Now, like I promised, here's a list of...what NOT to do when you're delegating (and later as well): *Do not tell the person how to do his job.*

Many entrepreneurs and managers have a compulsion to explain to the experts how to do their jobs. And the experts hate this habit. Don't fall into the trap of believing that you know how to do their job better. If you do know better, then you hired the wrong person.

Do not be too available

Most new-age entrepreneurs have the tendency of over-helping their people. This is a good thing, but I think that in some cases, helping is taken to an extreme. More precisely, if the person you delegated the task to calls you or emails you three times a day to ask about the delegated task, then that is unproductive. Tell your people that if they have questions, they should send them in one email per day. They don't get to call you. Why do you think I suggest this? Of course, if the problem is really important, they will call you. However, most of the time, the problems aren't that important or time sensitive, and they can solve them on their own.

Never make it personal

Don't assign work to employees on a personal level. Don't use phrases like 'Do this for me', 'I need to ask you a favour', 'This is important for me', or anything like this. I don't want to hit you over the head with this, but keep this in mind: *As long as that person is paid for his time and he does what he loves, he is not doing you any favour.* I don't intend to be mean, but if you don't take this suggestion seriously, you'll reach a point when you have a lot of people who have done a lot of favours for you that you'll have to repay in some way, and that's not good for anybody.

Never take the agreed-upon deadlines lightly

I'm not telling you to get mad at the person when he misses a deadline (again, don't take it personally), but what I want to say is that if you agreed to some consequences, stick to them. Otherwise, your employees will not take your deadlines seriously. For example, once an employee came to me and said that he couldn't do the task on time because someone in his family had died. This kind of situation will push you to the limit and will probably make you break your own rules. What I did, in that case, was to deduct the employee's salary by 50 per cent (as the previously agreed consequence), and then, I gave him a bonus of 100 per cent to cover the funeral arrangements.

Never fail to deliver on your promises

Keep 100 per cent of your promises that you make to your employees and maybe they will do the same. Keep 90 per cent of your promises and your employees will keep less than 50 per cent.

Follow these rules every time

It's like saying that you have read too many books and you don't need to read any more. Keep in mind that keeping the rules every time, no matter what, is more important for your employees than it is for yourself, because when you introduce exceptions, these will become the new norm.

Never fail to follow the delegation template for small tasks

Do you know how small tasks become big tasks? When you don't delegate them properly. If the task comes back to you done poorly or late, then that task will require double or triple the resources it needed in the first place.

Never change the rules because your employees don't like it at first

Nobody likes deadlines and consequences. If you are a leader, you have to live with that. Your job is not to be liked by your employees all the time; your job is to make your clients happy and push your employees past the limits they set for themselves. This is not an easy job, because if it were, everyone would do it.

TODAY's to-do list! (The best time to do it is NOW!)

1. Carefully reread the two lists that include things to do as well as things to avoid.

2. Take a piece of paper and rewrite the steps from the first list, then take some time to fully understand the motivations and implications of those stops.

3. Use this list during your next delegation meeting regardless of being at the receiving end of the delegation process.

Day 2

The Productive Refusal

*Don't let what you cannot do interfere
with what you can do.*
—JOHN WOODEN

In the previous lesson, we talked about an essential topic for any type of business that you're working on: Delegation. You received a list of things to do and things to avoid.

In this lesson, we're going to continue on the same path regarding professional relationships and we're going to talk about productive refusal.

The phrase may sound contradictory, but I chose it because it best expresses a reality that is guaranteed to increase your productivity.

One of the secrets of productivity, besides knowing what to put on your 'to-do' list, is the 'to-NOT-do' list, meaning the things you should refuse to do or stop doing.

A good metaphor for it is that *you can't drink wine from a glass filled with water. You first need to empty the glass of water before you can pour the wine into it.*

Similarly, if your schedule is filled with tasks that need to be done and that occupy a large part of your time, you can't introduce new activities that have a higher added value.

What I've noticed in many of my coaching sessions regarding productivity is that *too many people have tasks in their planner that were delegated to them—tasks they couldn't say 'no' to even though they weren't a part of their job description.*

And, not only did they not refuse the tasks at the opportune moment, they promised to deliver the results by setting completely unrealistic deadlines.

The consequence: They stopped doing what they set out to do (first- or second-level activities) to finish third-level tasks delegated by their superiors in a very short amount of time (see Priorities Pyramid).

This led to working overtime, family conflicts, not enough time for relaxation and so on and so forth.

All of these could have been avoided with a

Productive Refusal!

Let me show you exactly what I'm talking about.

How to practise it:

1. Never answer a request before first consulting your planner to check your already scheduled activities. Otherwise, be prepared to accept the consequences.

2. Offer deadline alternatives for the request you receive. Always take into account a safety margin to finish the tasks that are already planned.

3. When offering alternatives, keep in mind the level of the request. Allot time according to its level of priority (1 through 4).

4. Come to an agreement with all those who usually delegate tasks to you that for each delegated activity, they should allow you at least 24 hours to deliver the results. By doing this, you'll interrupt the pattern of 'putting out fires' constantly, a style of work that generates errors and results of mediocre quality.

5. Don't take responsibility for what you can't deliver at the requested time. Never accept a task using the words 'I'll try' because everybody in this situation will have something to lose:

    *   The person who delegates because he hopes it will be ready on time, and
    *   You, because you do whatever it takes and

consume a lot of resources whilst NOT finishing what you had planned as priorities!

To make the best decisions about these cases, take into account the list regarding the delegation process.

Be mindful of:

- 'Urgent' requests that don't involve you directly. Redirect those requests to the people right for the job.
- Co-workers who do not organize their time properly and end up passing on the task to others along with the stress involved. Be firm and don't let yourself be 'fooled' by the drama created by those who like to just put out fires. If you perpetuate the 'just this once' solution, it will be a surefire recipe for long-term failure.

TODAY's to-do list! (The best time to do it is NOW!)

1. Reread the rules for an effective and efficient delegation process.
2. Identify at least three situations in the past when you didn't practise 'the productive refusal' technique. What were the consequences? What would have happened if you had applied this principle then?
3. Remember at least three situations when you delegated

a task to someone else, and that person said they'll 'try' but failed to meet their deadline. What were the consequences you faced? Could you have done anything differently?

Day 3

You Failed. So What?

Vitality shows in not only the ability to persist but the ability to start over.
—F. SCOTT FITZGERALD

In the previous lesson, we talked about the productive refusal and how to finish what you set out to do without letting yourself get distracted by the 'pressing needs' of others.

Today we'll be discussing what you can do when, for some reason or another, you miss a day in your schedule.

What I recommend is the following *two-step sequence:*

Step 1: Forgive yourself!

Forgive yourself for not being 'perfect', because no one really is.

Step 2: Get back on the horse as soon as possible!

Restart the chain of good days as soon as possible.

Why is it important that you do so?

Small failures are almost inevitable, but herein lies the trap that most people who want to implement productive habits fall prey to.

They have a 'perfect' series for a few days, and then they fall off the wagon for one day. This is because they're not perfect anymore, they give up, feel disappointed and they plan to restart the process in a couple of days.

Unfortunately, for most people, this means they'll 'never' get back to what they were doing. The alternative to this is to accept 'the imperfection'. But under no circumstances should you let two consecutive days go by without practising the habit.

Starting over after just one break day is much easier than after two or more days.

Moreover, you need to update your 'WHY'. In other words, you need to reconnect the answer to the question, 'Why is doing this important to me?' and 'What values am I nourishing when I'm practising this habit?'

Most times, the simple act of rediscovering the relevance of an action you've come to practise out of a sense of inertia can offer you a consistent motivational boost.

It's like you've suddenly remembered you had a project with favourable future perspectives and you start massively reinvesting energy into it.

TODAY's to-do list! (The best time to do it is NOW!)

1. *'Clean' any negative emotion or regret* you might have regarding that day or those days you've missed. Promise yourself to be much more careful when practicing productive habits.

2. *Ask yourself,* 'Why is it important for me to implement these productive habits?' and 'What concrete benefits will I enjoy thirty days from now, six months from now or three years from now if I keep up these positive practices?'

Day 4

The Trait of Highly Intelligent People

How we spend our days is, of course, how we spend our lives.
—ANNIE DILLARD

In the previous lesson, we talked about how you can overcome failure and 'get back on the horse'. This is an essential factor for any medium and long-term project you wish to finish.

In this lesson, we'll be discussing an element that, when practised, *will decrease the likelihood of self-sabotage or falling off the wagon by at least 80 per cent!*

I'm talking about the daily revision.

Why is this activity so important?

This is because your mind relaxes when you allow it

the opportunity to draw the line after the experiences of the current day, to evaluate what worked and what didn't, and to capitalize on what it has learned.

Concretely, it's enough to ask some questions for five minutes. Don't be fooled by the fact that it's just five minutes.

It's probably the best five-minute investment you'll make all day. Even Socrates said, *'The unexamined life is not worth living!'*

These minutes will weigh heavily on your future successes because this is how you ensure growth and evolution by at least 1 per cent each day.

Here are the questions:

1. What worked today?
2. What didn't work today?
3. What have I learned today?
4. What will I do differently tomorrow?
5. What am I grateful for today?

TODAY's to-do list! (If you do this revision in the morning, use the previous day as a point of reference.)

1. Go through the list and answer the questions (preferably in the evening, an hour before you go to sleep).
2. For simplicity and organization purposes, it's best

that you use a notebook to write in daily. By doing so, you'll have all of the relevant information stored in one place.

Day 5

Slow as a Snail or
Fast as an Eagle?

Thinking is easy, acting is difficult, and to put one's thoughts into action is the most difficult thing in the world.

—GOETHE

In the previous lesson, we talked about how you can end your day in the best way possible. A day with closed loops is a prized day for sure!

I'll be approaching three distinct areas: email and PC, the Internet and online productivity tools.

Email and PC:

I have a couple of very clear rules I don't break because I know what that would mean for my productivity.

1. Inbox 0

This means that, at no point in time, will my inbox contain unread and unprocessed emails. Unfortunately, I know many people who leave all of their emails in their inbox, and when they need something, they just use 'search'.

I don't have a problem with finding a particular piece of information, but with the unconscious feeling of being overwhelmed that you experience when you open your inbox and see hundreds and thousands of emails—read or unread—it becomes irksome. To me, it is the same feeling like having a couple of reams of paper placed chaotically on my desk. I suggest you create themed folders (clients, suppliers, administrator, personal, accounting, marketing, sales, John, Mary, etc.) Almost any type of sorting is better than none!

The feeling of having an empty inbox is priceless! It's a liberating feeling because you know nothing will evade your keen eye now, contrary to those moments when you have to sort through hundreds of read or unread emails…Try it out and we'll talk afterwards.

2. **If it's a level 1 or 2 email, answer it instantly** (during the Pomodoro dedicated to networking).

   If it's a level 3 or 4, then postpone answering it and place it at the end of your priorities list.

3. **Prioritize to answer those emails where you're in the 'TO:' field because they are directly addressed to you, but use the 1–4 ranking for priorities.**

   Leave the emails where you're in the 'CC:' field for later on and completely ignore those where you're in the 'BCC:' field.

4. **Your desktop should have 80–100 per cent free space.** You should be able to see the background picture without icons on it.

   It's the same principle as the one for Inbox 0. Crowded icons instantaneously increase your stress level. Do yourself a favour and clean your desktop often to have peace of mind.

5. **The ratio between folders and files should be a maximum of 5-to-1** (Word, Excel, etc.)

   Your desktop should only contain the file you're currently working on or the one you use daily.

   Why? This is because it would mean that your files are sorted and not just crammed everywhere on your desktop.

   In any case, if you have more than five folders on your desktop, I highly doubt your organization capabilities and discipline.

Concentrate the information using a maximum of five folders. Ideally, you should use one to three folders. You'll immediately feel like you're more in control over what you have to do.

The Internet

1. **Personal email, Facebook and other similar applications are only allowed during the 5-minute break after your Pomodoro session.**
   It's absolutely critical, for your professional life, NOT to start your workday with your reward. Start with working hard for your important projects and only afterwards reward yourself.

2. **Your relaxation time should never be longer than the allotted time!**
   If you've decided something, discipline yourself to respect your decisions. If you break your promises, your self-esteem will drop fairly quickly. However, when you keep the promises you make to yourself, your self-confidence increases.

3. **To determine exactly how much time you're wasting on the Internet, you could use the Rescue Time App (https://www.rescuetime.com/).**
   It's a software that monitors your desktop and determines your level of productivity throughout the

day. I still experience 'A-ha!' moments and continue to use it. I promise this app will provide a sudden jolt back to reality for some people.

Online productivity tools

1. **Evernote** (https://evernote.com/)
   It's my #1 favourite. I'm even writing this on Evernote, a software that can be synchronized online with any type of device from your PC or Mac. It also works with Windows, iOS and iPhone because it's compatible with computers, tablets and smartphones.

   Evernote is a database hosted on a server where you can organize all of the information you need.

   It gives me the peace of mind I need because I know that even if my computer, phone or tablet were to break down, my information would be safe. Twice in my life I have lost everything on my computer and I've felt the pain both physically and mentally. I'm glad to get rid of this stress factor.

2. **Dropbox** (https://www.dropbox.com/)
   It's the best file-sharing software.

   When you're working on projects where you collaborate with someone else, it helps especially when you don't have to send that person large files by email and interrupt them in their productive Pomodoro sessions.

3. **WeTransfer** (https://www.wetransfer.com/)

   It's the best file transferring software.

   I really like it because it's fast, you can transfer up to 2GB of data and your files are kept on their servers for one week.

   Of course, there are many other apps and programmes that help out, but the ones mentioned above constitute the necessary and sufficient minimum through which you can increase your online productivity.

TODAY's to-do list! (The best time to do it is NOW!)

1. Reread the list and decide what you can implement right away, over the course of just one Pomodoro session (for instance, identify the 3–5 folders, move the desktop files you're not using anymore, sort your inbox, etc.). Go for these quick victories!

2. Establish a set of personal rules regarding your interaction with the online environment for entertainment purposes—how long, how often, when during the day, etc. For this practice to work even better, find someone who wants to implement a similar shift to yours and monitor each other once per day.

3. Allot one Pomodoro session to explore the three pieces of software—Evernote, Dropbox and WeTransfer (if

you're not using them already). For each one, you'll find a presentation video and/or instructions. Start using them even if you don't know ALL the details (be careful not to self-sabotage yourself).

Day 6

Recharge and Prepare (Part IV)

Don't say you don't have enough time. You have exactly the same number of hours per day that were given to Helen Keller, Pasteur, Michelangelo, Mother Teresa, Leonardo da Vinci, Thomas Jefferson, and Albert Einstein.

—H. JACKSON BROWN JR.

This fourth week has come to a close!

I'm curious about how you have evolved, what challenges you had faced and what 'A-ha!' moments you've had.

Okay, let's see what you've learned this week.

Day 22: Delegating with spectacular results!

Essential idea:

You've learned about an elaborate but spectacularly effective delegation process. It might seem stuffy, but once you go through it 3–4 times, it will become easier. It will actually become harder not to follow it!

Day 23: The productive refusal

Essential idea:

A simple technique and yet it has the potential to increase your productivity many times over. If you don't implement it, you have every chance of remaining the 'professional fireman' who puts out fires in the office.

Day 24: How do you get over failure?

Essential idea:

You've learned the two-step process through which you overcome failure. You've also reminded yourself that without a 'why' you can't get 'where' you want to.

Day 25: Daily revision

Essential idea:

You received five 'golden' questions that will help you learn something new daily and help you evolve step-by-step in a predictable manner. It only takes five minutes to ask yourself these questions but their cumulative effects will already be taking place after only a couple of weeks.

Day 26: Online productivity: email, Internet and productivity tools

Essential idea:

Maintaining your online productivity level has become a great challenge considering all the distractions that are out there. Follow my advice and use the pieces of software I recommended to remain effective and efficient.

Okay, now *let's see how well you fared after your fourth week:*

1. On how many days (out of 5), did you practise the exercise for each lesson? (0-5) >
2. How many minutes, on an average, did it take you to complete the daily exercise? >
3. What topic from this fourth week have you found most relevant or revealing? Why? >
4. How happy are you with the progress you've made? (1 – not happy at all; 10 – very happy) What was required to happen so that your score would have been 1–2 points higher? >

5. How dedicated are you to continue to improve your level of organization and discipline? (1 – not at all; 10 – very dedicated) >

Day 7

A Burning-hot Desire

The greatest saleswoman in the world today does not mind if you call her a girl. That is because Markita Andrews has generated more than eighty thousand dollars selling Girl Scout cookies since she was seven years old.

Going door-to-door after school, the shy Markita transformed herself into a cookie-selling dynamo when she discovered, at age thirteen, the secret of selling.

It starts with desire, A BURNING HOT DESIRE.

For Markita and her mother, who worked as a waitress in New York after her husband left them when Markita was eight years old, their dream was to travel the globe. 'I will work hard to make enough money to send you to college,' her mother said one day. 'You'll go to college and graduate, you will make enough money to take you and me around the world. Okay?'

So at age 13 when Markita read in her Girl Scout magazine that the Scout who sold the most cookies would win an all-expenses-paid trip for two around the world, *she decided to sell all the Girl Scout cookies she could— more Girl Scout cookies than anyone in the world, ever.*

But desire alone was not enough to make her dream come true. Markita knew she needed a plan.

'Always wear your right outfit, your professional garb,' her aunt advised. 'When you are doing business, dress like you are doing business. Wear your Girl Scout uniform. When you go up to people in their tenement buildings at 4:30 or 6:30, and especially on a Friday night, ask for a big order. Always smile—whether they buy or not, always be nice. And don't ask them to buy your cookies; ask them to invest.'

Many other scouts may have wanted that trip around the world. Lots of other scouts may have had a plan. But only Markita went after her *dream* in her uniform each day. 'Hi, I have a dream. I am earning a trip around the world for me and my mom by merchandising Girl Scout cookies,' she would say at the door. 'Would you like to invest in one dozen or two dozen boxes of cookies?'

Markita sold 3,526 boxes of Girl Scout cookies that year and won her trip around the world.

Since then, she has sold more than 42,000 boxes of Girl Scout cookies, spoken at sales conventions across the country, starred in a Disney movie about her adventure and has co-authored the bestseller, *How To Sell More Cookies, Condos, Cadillacs, Computers…and Everything Else.*

Markita is no smarter and no more extroverted than thousands of other people, young and old, with dreams of their own. The big difference is, Markita has discovered the secret of selling: i.e. ASK, ASK, ASK!

Many people fail before they even begin because they fail to ask for what they want. The fear of rejection leads many of us to reject our dreams and ourselves long before anyone else ever has the chance, no matter what we are selling.

'Actually everyone is selling something in a way. You are selling yourself every day—in school, to your boss, to new people you meet,' said Markita at 14. 'My mother is a waitress—she sells the daily special. Mayors and presidents trying to get votes are selling… One of my teachers, who made geography so very interesting to her students, was really selling to her class. I see selling everywhere I look and selling is part of the whole world.'

It takes courage to ask for what you want. Courage is not the absence of fear. It's doing what it takes, despite one's fear. And, as Markita discovered, the more you ask, the easier it gets and it is also more fun.

Once, on live TV, the producer decided to give Markita her toughest selling challenge. Markita was asked to sell Girl Scout cookies to another guest on the show. 'Would you like to invest in one dozen or two dozen boxes of Girl Scout cookies?' she asked.

'Girl Scout cookies? I don't buy any Girl Scout cookies,' he replied. 'I am a Federal Penitentiary Warden. I put 2,000 rapists, robbers, criminals, muggers and child abusers to bed every night.'

Unruffled, Markita quickly countered, 'Mister, if you take some of these cookies, maybe you won't be so mean and angry and evil. And, Mister, I think it would be a good idea for you to take some of these cookies back for every one of your 2,000 prisoners too,' Markita said.

The warden wrote a cheque.

Moral: The only real limits are the ones we create in our mind!

THE FINISH

Day 1

Sweating in Training or
Bleeding in Battle?

Spectacular achievement is always preceded by unspectacular preparation.

—ROBERT SCHULLER

'Mrs Jenkins,' the grade school teacher, announced to Stuart's mother, 'your son will never graduate from high school, let alone attend college. It's because of his dyslexia—you see, he's learning disabled.' Stuart sat in the slow class, the one-room schoolhouse in a little town, Nebraska, where everyone knew everyone. The worst part was not that the town labelled him 'dumb' and 'stupid'. The worst part was that Stuart believed the labels. Until, that is, the day that everything changed for him.

When Stuart reached junior-high age, he was given the opportunity to attend private school away from home, and it was there that the earlier labels that had been placed on him would gradually disappear. Not only did he become the school's track star and champion runner, but the confidence he gained also helped him distinguish himself academically.

Contrary to the earlier predictions, he not just graduated high school, but he became student body president and went on to graduate college with a 3.2 grade point average. And all because of his very unique concept of the word 'discipline'. Stuart's love for running prompted him to set a long-range goal: to qualify for the Olympic trials by running the Boston Marathon in two hours, nineteen minutes and four seconds!

Beginning at age fifteen, every single day for eight years, Stuart ran in preparation for that great race. He did not miss one day in eight years! Would you say that was discipline? In fact, by the time Stuart reached Boston, his daily log indicated he had run exactly 26,000 miles in preparation for that one 26-mile race! That's 1,000 miles of preparation for every mile in the race! Here are his own words about what happened as he ran in the Boston marathon:

Everything was going great until I got to the 17-mile mark–Heartbreak Hill, as it's affectionately called. It was as if somebody had turned on burners under both my heels and I had 4-inch blisters on them. My shoes were full of blood. There was more pain than I could ever remember in my life. I had to ask myself, am I willing to take one more step on these feet? Then the answer came: 'Stuart you are within six miles of reaching the goal you set eight years ago. The goal you have pursued for 26,000 miles!' And the power of the goal was much greater than the power of the pain. I kept going, climbing the next hill.

As I reached the crest of the hill, I looked out and saw a huge digital clock. It read: TWO HOURS, EIGHTEEN MINUTES, FORTY-SIX SECONDS. That meant only one thing. I had just eighteen seconds to get from there to the finish line! Then I heard a voice on the loudspeaker: Ladies and gentlemen, here comes Stuart Jenkins. He's the last runner who has a chance to qualify for the Olympic trials. Let's bring him on in. Twenty thousand people jumped to their feet and began cheering wildly. But my entire focus was on that digital clock! Tick. Tick. Tick. I'm not a sprinter, but I believe I actually sprinted for the finish line, and in just fourteen seconds I was there, qualifying for the Olympics—by just FOUR SECONDS![1]

Now ask yourself, which day should Stuart Jenkins have skipped in his training? Which day should he have allowed himself not to pursue his goal? What mile in those 26,000 miles of preparation should he not have run? What does the word 'discipline' mean? It means freedom! It's not putting yourself in a box; it's putting yourself on top of the box, giving yourself a structure that can support you. The box is not a trap, a confinement or a prison cell. It's a platform, a solid step that affords you a higher vantage point from which to view your possibilities. Eight years of running every single day—that was discipline for Stuart Jenkins. But that kind of discipline is what gives you freedom, freedom from mediocrity!

Think of discipline as the path to freedom—freedom from limitations! Clearly define your goal and focus on it. Don't let yourself quit too soon. And when you hit your 'Heartbreak Hill', keep going!

[1]www.mindperk.com/articles/discipline-the-path-to-freedom/, accessed on 30 November 2018.

Day 2

Highlights of the Journey

Smile, breathe and go slowly.
—THICH NHAT HANH

In this lesson, we have a very important activity to go through.

I'm talking about a recap so that you become very aware of the tools you received and the 'technical specifications' that came with them.

Before I begin, let me tell what my intention was when I created this book. First of all, *I wanted to lend you a helping hand with everything that's already going on in your life.* I'm talking about work tasks, home chores and anything else that fills your day.

My intention was to help you 'make room' for new and important activities by increasing your productivity expressed through effectiveness and efficiency.

You have to finish what you've already started so it's completely unrealistic for me to tell you to 'stop doing what you have to do, just do these things'. So:

Step 1: Organization and discipline with regard to what already exists. You've already taken out some time and have the energy for more important activities—1st and 2nd level from the Priority Pyramid.

Step 2: Clarify your destination and then go down the road in a well-organized and disciplined manner. To successfully accomplish this second step, my next book will be about 'The Strategic Life Planning'. But let's begin the recap:

We started the first week by talking about motivations. We spoke about 'why discipline and organization are important'.

I helped you gain access to the habits of successful people and I invited you to find your motivations.

You created your definitions for these two concepts and evaluated your starting point with the help of fifteen questions regarding personal discipline.

Then, we discussed the tension that arises between

motivations and fears hidden in the form of excuses. And together, we saw that when you have a higher purpose for doing something, overcoming obstacles becomes easier.

During the second week, we concentrated on what could slow you down or stop you from becoming more organized and disciplined.

The first step was getting to know the three enemies of organization and discipline: 'Frequent interruptions', 'Start and Stop' and 'Unrelated activities'.

We then continued with the criteria through which you establish your daily priorities. The Priorities Pyramid is an extraordinary tool that you can use to figure out, at any given time, if you're using your time and energy in the best possible way.

The next step was to 'dust off' the old paradigms that slowed you down and adopt the new ones used by top performers.

Later, we talked about balance and harmony and how they can be achieved through nourishing your four intelligences.

We ended the week with the open loops audit, or how I like to call it 'the Terminator of black holes that destroys personal energy'.

During the third week, I revealed to you ways in which you can increase your productivity.

I began with order as a daily natural working state.

We then covered the Pomodoro technique, which is one of the top three best productive methods there is.

We continued with training your ability to concentrate in five simple steps. We concluded the week with simple ways in which you can collect ideas and tasks, grouping them afterwards in blocks and executing them in an optimum sequence of Pomodoro sessions.

And, last but not least, we agreed that the first part of your day (30–120 minutes) should be reserved for strategic thinking and planning the day ahead.

During the fourth week, we added some more essential resources to complete the arsenal of tools that make life easier and more pleasant.

We started with the demystification of the delegation process. There are many ways to delegate, but only a few of them actually work. Delegate in a proper manner and you'll make your life easier. Also, if something is being delegated to you, make sure the perfect context is created for you to perform while doing that activity.

We continued with 'productive refusal' and ways to overcome failure. Another essential element for organization and discipline that we talked about was the daily revision. Those five minutes you allot in the evening will make a huge difference for you in the months and years to come. It may not seem like a lot but the cumulative effect is impressive!

And, we concluded the week with a few ideas and suggestions on how to approach the complex virtual world in an organized and disciplined fashion. It has become quite easy for you to get distracted and then 'wake up' after 'being on a different planet' for hours.

All of these tools complement each other and help you stay organized, disciplined and productive day after day.

I want to resume what I said in the beginning. This book has a lot of top instruments to help you increase your organization and discipline. But, even more than that, *I believe they help you structure your mind differently.*

This new way allows you to obtain clarity, energy, self-confidence and significance. In other words, it allows you to nourish all four of your intelligences. Like I said, *I wanted to help you 'see the light' in your life.*

And, after you've stabilized yourself, I wanted to help you plan your next destination not because 'you have to' or 'there's no other choice' but because 'it's your choice' without being pressured by external factors.

Organization and discipline are synonymous with taking your power back and becoming the master of your life again, day after day.

I don't know if there are any sensations that are more unpleasant than the one where you feel you're losing control over your life and getting carried away.

This is why I ask you to study and apply organization and discipline. Transform them into daily practices and your life is sure to get better.

I'm here for you if you have any questions or need more information.

Have a productive day!

Day 3

How to Avoid the
Rubber Band Effect!

You don't have to be great to start,
but you have to start to be great.

—JOE SABAH

We have now reached the end of this journey that promises to bring you generous benefits in the weeks, months and years to come.

Thank you for trusting me to be your guide throughout this exploration!

I trust you have received valuable information during these days, and you have developed essential abilities that can be used for a long time from here onwards...and who knows? Maybe forever!

I have a firm belief, not just for this context, that each ending is, in fact, an opportunity to begin a new exploration from a higher step.

In other words, we evolve, but from a different level of understanding things. And this continuous evolution is one of the characteristics of happiness from the way I understand life.

During the next couple of days, it would help you greatly to revise certain themes and ingrain what you've found to be useful. It's an opportunity to transform the changes you've begun to implement into permanent ones.

When implementing change, 'the rubber band theory' applies.

When you start to make concrete changes, you're distancing yourself from the place you once were.

However, the inertia of the system you're a part of will oppose these changes by creating 'tension'.

It's like holding a rubber band with one finger and pulling its head with another finger.

The rubber band wears thin but most of the times it has the ability to pull you back.

In these cases, to stabilize the shift and make it permanent, you need to do something as many times as it takes to 'break the rubber band'; in other words, until the inertia of 'what was' is overcome and 'what is' becomes stable in its newest form and context.

This is why consistent practice is so important... If you don't create momentum to break the rubber band, it will pull you back and nullify any type of progress.

I wish you the best of luck!

P.S.: I would love to hear from you! While it's easy to connect over Facebook, Twitter or other social media sites; often it's better to have one-on-one conversations with readers like you.

So I encourage you to reach out over email and say hi!

Simply write here: dan@5amcoaching.com

You can also check my website, http://www.5amhacks.com.

To get started, I would love to hear about the one thing you'll do...this week...to turn this information into action.

Could you help?

Before you go, I'd like to say 'thank you' for purchasing my book.

I know you could have picked from dozens of books on productivity or habit development, but you took a chance with my system.

I'd love to hear your opinion about my book. In the world of book publishing, there are few things more valuable than honest reviews from a wide variety of readers.

Your review will help other readers find out whether my book is for them or not. It will also help me reach more readers by increasing the visibility of the book.

You can leave your review on the Amazon. I will very much appreciate it!

One more thing...

Make sure you also read my first published book—*The 5 A.M. Revolution: Why High Achievers Wake Up Early and How You Can Do It Too*—that reached *#1 spot on Amazon worldwide in the Time Management Section* and stayed there for several weeks.

THE EXTRAS:
5 SUPER POWERS
TO BE USED DAILY

1

The Anti-procrastination Silver Bullet

I sometimes hear a voice inside my head, and this voice... it negotiates with me!

Has anything similar ever happened to you?

I think it has, but don't worry, it's just your internal dialogue.

What's curious about this voice is that, in 95 per cent of the cases, it negotiates the terms of the contract of the things I want to do against my higher interest!

How does this happen?

The answer is simple—for example, it negotiates that it would be okay for me to eat another piece of cake or sleep for another ten minutes after the alarm clock went off or to watch another episode (the third in a row) of my favourite TV series and so on.

Okay, so maybe you're telling yourself, 'But I feel so good when I do all of these things.'

And, I agree with you, you do feel good, for a short amount of time.

This is because *every time you choose to do one thing, you automatically choose NOT to do another thing at the same time.*

I'm going to repeat this phrase because it's very important: Every time you choose to do one thing, you automatically choose NOT to do another thing at the same time.

So why is this phrase so important? This is because:

- when you eat that third piece of cake, you actually choose not to care about your weight
- when you sleep for another ten minutes, you actually choose to skip breakfast and thus start your day without the necessary amount of energy
- when you play a video game after you arrived at home, you choose not to speak with your spouse and connect after a long day being apart.

Every choice you make has its consequences, either good or bad.

You might be telling yourself right now: 'So what, can't a person indulge themselves once in a while?'

I'm glad you brought this up!

Herein lies your greatest challenge: when it happens more than once and when it happens consistently.

I'm talking about a consistency that in time will stop you from moving forward, or even worse…it will pull you back into your old routine.

If you want to have a stronger negotiating position with this inner voice of yours that successfully manages to negotiate in your detriment (in the long run), I propose that you implement the following solution:

The idea came to me about three years ago when I was obsessed with exercising consistently.

While going through this process, I had days when I managed to achieve what I set out to do and days when I banged my head against the wall.

This was very frustrating for me because, if I skipped 3–4 days of exercising, it was very difficult for me to get back in the saddle and to overcome my inertia. I needed at least 2–3 days to get started with my exercises on the fourth day.

Moreover, my muscles responded negatively every time I would start exercising after a break through cramps and pains that made me become even more aware of my inconsistency.

Until one day when I said, 'Enough is enough! I can't go on like this!'

So I asked myself the following question: How much time am I willing to invest every day to practice my physical exercises routine?

'Well…about 45 minutes.'

Aha…okay…what would be the minimum amount of time I could spend exercising that would spare me the muscle cramps and discomfort I experience when I restart exercising after my passive periods?

'Well…10–15 minutes.'

Aha…very interesting! So, somewhere between a quarter up to a third of the ideal time spent, approximately 25–33 per cent of the ideal.

That was the moment when something inside of me yelled: '10–15 minutes of daily exercise is feasible!' And that's when I felt a sense of internal relaxation.

That's when I told myself that, from now onwards, whether it's raining or windy, whether I'm on a vacation or travelling for business, I will exercise for at least 10 minutes every day.

Will I exercise for JUST 10 minutes EACH day?

No! Depending on how I feel I will exercise longer, BUT I will respect this minimum.

In the long run, this practice will make a huge difference, because it's much easier to maintain a habit which uses up just my level three or four type of energy (on a scale of one to ten) than continually restarting my exercise programme and consuming a level eight or nine type of energy to overcome my inertia!

I'm also convinced that you already know that only practice makes perfect as well as positive habits practised consistently!

Okay, so how can you apply this method to any context in your life?

How can you implement positive habits using a minimum amount of effort?

Adopt a non-negotiable strategy, based on the minimal accepted level of action. Decide:

- The minimum number of steps you'll take each day to lose weight
- The minimum number of pages you'll read daily to increase your expertise
- The minimum number of minutes you'll spend with your family
- The minimum number of glasses of water you'll drink throughout the day
- The minimum number of minutes you'll spend planning and prioritizing your activities for a specific day

And these are just a few ideas, but start with a single mini-habit.

Establish the ideal towards which you strive, but begin

by feeling okay to achieve just a quarter or a third of that ideal.

I guarantee you'll have a lot more days when you'll get closer to your ideal if you establish this non-negotiable minimum rather than if you don't, because, as one law of physics reminds us, a moving object tends to stay in motion, and a static object tends to remain still.

And this is what I wish for you as well, to keep going, and, with each step you take, to get closer and closer to what you want.

Live remarkably and transform each day into an extraordinary one! Welcome to the unlimited world of all that you can be!

2

The Victory Chain

It's so easy to lose sight of the progress we have made, especially when our mind is solely focused on the finish line, measuring the distance we still have to go.

This is exactly the difference between perfection and progress!

You can measure your actions through the lens of perfection and feel constantly dissatisfied because you find out how far from perfection your actions are, or, you can measure your progress day by day, week by week, year by year and celebrate it!

Celebrate the fact that you're 1 per cent better than the person you were yesterday and that today you're doing everything you can so that come tomorrow, you will be

1 per cent better than you were today.

Since I realized, how important it is to constantly measure one's progress—precisely because it charges one with the energy of certainty, the certainty that one is on the right track and getting closer and closer to one's destination—I found the antidote for frustration and discontentment arising once I started using perfection as the standard by which I judged the quality of my actions.

Courtesy of Jerry Seinfeld and his genius method, now anyone can instantaneously track and visualize their progress and smile.

Better still, anyone will be able to more easily get over their poor moods, their feelings of laziness, procrastination tendencies or even just a simple day during which their level of energy is low...and still accomplish what they set out to do... This is because they don't want to break the victory chain they have created until that moment.

The method is called 'Don't break the chain', but I think it sounds much better if we name it 'The Victory Chain'.

Essentially, what you have to do to practise this habit like a professional is to:

1. Establish the goal or habit you wish to monitor
2. Figure out a daily, non-negotiable minimum
3. Firmly establish the exceptions
4. Print out a calendar or use the template that I

provide at the end of this method

5. Buy a big red marker, place it near your calendar and draw a big 'X' for every day you accomplish what you set out to do.

A few notes:

The concept of a non-negotiable minimum is explained in the previous lesson.

Firmly establishing the exceptions: This relates to those very rare situations (1 per cent) when you allow yourself to not even accomplish the non-negotiable minimum. These exceptions are set out from the beginning and you can't abdicate from them.

For example:

- I'm going to a wedding, I can't wake up at 5 a.m. the next day.
- I have a fever and a cold, I can't exercise for 15 minutes that day.
- I'm away on a business trip, I can't spend time with my family.

Very important!

Think about these exceptions very carefully and finish the list BEFORE you begin your journey to reach a goal or start practising a habit. It's completely counterproductive to introduce exceptions later on—that will only act against you—once you have started your practice.

In conclusion, print a calendar or the template at the end of the lesson and start monitoring your progress, whether it's about the Morning Routine, the Daily Review or other new habit that you want to implement.

You can also monitor a sub-category that is part of a much larger habit you wish to implement. For example, 15 minutes of physical exercise daily, waking up at 5 a.m., establishing your top three priorities for the day, etc.

Victory Chain   5AM Victory Chain by Dan Luca

Date	HABIT						
	M	T	W	T	F	S	S
	M	T	W	T	F	S	S
	M	T	W	T	F	S	S
	M	T	W	T	F	S	S
	M	T	W	T	F	S	S
	M	T	W	T	F	S	S

3

Micro Dose for Mega Results

I'm receiving the following question more and more often:

'I make time for the things I don't like but *have* to do, and still, I don't do them. It's like an invisible force is holding me in place. Can you help me?'

And I usually ask them: 'Are you referring to cleaning up your desk, calling your prospects, apologizing after you've made a mistake, going to the gym consistently, waking up in the morning as soon as the alarm goes off?'

'Yes, yes, all of those things!' they answer, almost without exception.

Five years ago, I would have probably shrugged my shoulders and said, 'Well, just start your day with these activities and one day you'll figure it out,' but now I don't say this anymore because I've realized this method works for just 10–20 per cent of the people who were asking me for advice.

For the other 80–90 per cent, I am convinced that *the best solution is 'micro-productivity'*.

Why do I believe this to be true?

This is because this 80–90 per cent of people has a very low tolerance for pain or discomfort!

Then, it's like pulling out a tooth or ripping off a band-aid. You need a swift and precise movement so your 'resistance' won't be activated as much.

And micro-productivity does just that: it takes an essentially unpleasant activity, compresses it into a very short time period, and delivers a lasting result with a minimum of associated pain.

For me, this method turned out to be a real revelation once I started noticing that the activities I had tried so hard to avoid were 'tamed' when they were compressed into short term intervals.

To make micro-productivity a viable option for myself, I avoided, at any cost, thinking 'I'll do this thing until it's finished', because then it would have taken me an eternity!

Instead, I held 'an internal meeting' during which I made sure I had the necessary energy, the required level of clarity over how I was going to act, enough self-confidence to see this activity through to the end and an obvious understanding of why this effort would help me.

Having all of these resources aligned with the activity that I was to undertake turned my 10-minute 'sprint' into a success 95 per cent of the time!

If you're facing many such challenging activities, you can proceed as follows:

1. Allot 1 hour for five of your least desired activities you've been putting off for days or weeks.

2. Plan five 10-minute sessions—one session for each challenge—with a 2-minute break between them. If you finish an activity in less than 10 minutes, take the 2-minute break and then start the next one.

3. Execute these activities in 'rapid fire' mode and free yourself of the pressure you've been carrying around.

4. If you give it your all and still don't manage to finish a certain task…celebrate! You've just made significant progress and you'll most likely need just another 10-minute session to finish that activity.

5. Award yourself for 'slaying the dragon' that was disturbing your peace!

Let's see what type of activities can be dealt with using these 10-minute sprints:

- Let's say you have to call your supplier and tell him you're going to be late with the payment. It's only natural that this call doesn't come easy for you, making you want to postpone it indefinitely, for fear of ruining a good relationship.

- Then, let's assume you want to go for a check-up to investigate some symptoms you've been experiencing. You could also be experiencing fear regarding the probable causes…and, as you already know, it's easier to just ignore the signs than it is to thoroughly investigate them. And no, I don't agree with the saying: 'Ignorance is bliss.'

- Another example of a difficult activity could be updating your record of weekly or monthly expenses. This could reveal the fact that you've gone overbudget, spent money on nonsense or that you don't have enough money left to save the 10 per cent you wanted to.

- Maybe you need to call one of your parents to apologize for snapping at them on the phone yesterday when they called you right before an important meeting. Most of us find it difficult to accept our mistakes and take the first step towards reconciliation. Unfortunately, they are guided by the erroneous principle that 'time heals all wounds'.

Of course, there are probably 1,000 other activities that are fit for these micro-productivity sprints, however, I believe these examples have helped you get an idea about the fact that we mostly postpone the things that can cause us emotional discomfort.

Also, it is a fact that this emotional discomfort will probably increase if the 'necessary' activity is not performed as soon as possible.

All of the examples mentioned above may cause you great short-term discomfort, but they have the potential to prevent far worse situations that could take place in the future:

- **Not calling your supplier to inform him that you'll be late with the payment**: You'll surely end up paying penalties, your contract might be suspended or the supplier could sue you
- **Not going for your check-up:** You miss detecting the problem in its earlier stage and, from some point onwards, nothing can be done for your health
- **Not keeping your expenses under control:** You'll wake up penniless, you'll end up borrowing money, living from one paycheck to the next, feeling stressed, getting sick a lot...
- **Not apologizing to your parents when you've made a mistake:** They will be affected by this

(they're probably old, as well) and your behaviour could cause a deterioration of their health. It could make them feel that their own children are ungrateful or they could have other similar negative perceptions. All of these are very stressful, emotionally, especially during old age.

Of course, this 'emotional discomfort' is just a kinder way of saying you're AFRAID!

And the muscle that deals with fear has been weakened in most people's cases...because it hasn't faced its challenges at their proper time, and the consequences have become increasingly more serious and the fight is now unbalanced.

But what I want to tell you is that you can take your POWER back! How?

Through guerrilla warfare!

Short periods of time when you face your fear, create a ten-minute ambush, gain a victory and retreat!

Fear can regroup quite quickly, but when it comes to actions that take less than ten minutes, the resistance is less strong.

Thus, with every battle you win, your 'courage' muscle strengthens, your 'self-confidence' rises and, slowly but surely, you'll find yourself fighting even greater fears, and then you'll realize that your comfort zone has been extended without you even noticing it.

Therefore, award yourself the daily present of at least one ten-minute session when you look fear in the eye, do the uncomfortable and give yourself the chance to become the best version of yourself!

4

Refresh P.M.

Waking up early in the morning has a lot of advantages, but it also have some drawbacks.

One of the drawbacks is the fact that around noon, the energy level drops and you might experience a period of sleepiness.

In order to maintain your productivity and have a high level of energy even in the middle of the day, I will give you a synthesis technique called Refresh P.M.

It came up as a solution during one of my coaching sessions, and I realized how useful it is, especially because it deals with an issue that's probably challenging for you as well.

This technique allows you to push the restart button

in the middle of the day!

Namely, after you've woken up at 5 a.m. and finished your routine to gain more energy, clarity and meaning, you leap towards the start of the day. But after 12 p.m...1 p.m...2 p.m...a feeling of fatigue starts enveloping you and your physical and mental tonus starts decreasing.

What can you do?

I'm going to offer you two 30-minute options that can reset your energy level and help you increase it by 25–50 per cent.

If you're already using the Pomodoro technique, the 30-minute break after the four sessions is just right for one of these two options.

The best time interval to practise REFRESH P.M. is probably between 1 p.m. and 3 p.m.

So, let's see what you can do, specifically:

Option 1: 30 minutes (focus on your physical energy)

This option is subject to your context, meaning, it's necessary that you have a conducive environment, you'll see why:

1. **20 minutes—Power nap:** You need to set your alarm to go off after 20 minutes (tops!) so you wake up before you enter deep sleep. These 20 minutes are enough!

   I have been practising this mini-habit for the last three years and every day I have felt the incredible refreshing effect it has!

2. **2 minutes—Wash your face with cold water:** It has a special effect: it will wake you up very fast!

3. **1 minute—2 glasses of water (at body temperature):** Approx. 16 oz/0.5 litre

4. **2 minutes—Deep breathing:** A minimum of five repetitions during which you inhale for eight seconds and then exhale for eight seconds

5. **2 minutes—1 or 2 raw and juicy fruits:** Preferably ones you need to chew—apples, pears, peaches, etc.

6. **3 minutes**—Stretching and massaging your face and scalp (including your eyes, ears and the back of your head)

This is awesome because in this way you win another 4–5 hours of high productivity instead of dragging through the remaining day.

Option 2: 30 minutes (focus on all of the four intelligences)

1. **20 minutes**—If you can't sleep, go for a 20-minute walk, preferably somewhere green where you can relax, destress and clear your mind.

2. **5 minutes—Mindfulness:** Scan your internal state and, using your breathing, relax any part of your body that feels tense.

3. **4 minutes**—Be grateful for all the good things in your

life and acknowledge all the people that are part of your life.

4. **1 minute—Affirmations:** Say to yourself ten times— 'I am energetic, I am focused, I am confident and I have a purpose. I am kind, I am generous and I am grateful to live my life.'

If you only have a couple of minutes to spare, combine as many of the short activities as you can so that you obtain a result that's as close as possible to the one you want!

Enjoy it!

5

Magical Evening Recipe

Productivity is not an accident or an unpredictable event!

Productivity can be predictable, provided you treat it as a continuum and not as a singular event.

In other words, you should be focusing on productivity from the moment you wake up, until you go to bed. And, I will tell you how to get ready in the evening so you have a productive next day.

You've already practised Daily Review and reaped the rewards. Now it's important that we prepare for the following day, considering all of the four intelligences (body, mind, emotions and soul).

I'm writing about this subject to provide an alternative to what unfortunately happens in too many families.

He's dead tired after a hard day at work and takes refuge in front of the TV, to unwind his over utilized neurons.

She comes home and starts her second shift. She still has to clean, wash, take care of the kids, and if there's any time left, she takes care of herself.

Both his and her needs are legitimate, but I truly believe that there's another way, because I've experienced it for myself as well as seen other people experience it.

And this 'other way', if it's practised on a daily basis, will generate a significant improvement in the quality of life of every member in the family (including your kids) in a relatively short amount of time.

So, what I suggest is that you revise your evening schedule and implement as many activities as you can from the following 15 practices:

1. **Allow yourself at least 30 minutes to 'land' quietly at home after your daily turmoil.** Create a routine that will predictably help you reach the best state for a restful sleep. Most children already have a routine for going to bed and this helps them fall asleep a lot easier. We, grown-ups, have apparently forgotten the benefits of this type of routine that will allow our mind to slow down its frantic rhythm.

2. **Set your alarm to go off at 10 p.m.** To let you know that you have just 30 minutes left to fall asleep and that it's time you start your 'smooth falling asleep' routine.

   What are the things that could help you relax and fall asleep much easier as soon as you get into bed? If you still don't have a plan, it's possible to find inspiration reading the ideas below.

3. **Savour a cup of jasmine tea.** Drinking your tea in quiet can offer you a sense of calm and relaxation that is extremely suitable and compatible with restful sleep. You can also drink a cup of linden tea or a glass of warm milk with honey. What's important is that you savour this drink and relax your body.

4. **Listen to relaxing music.** This could also be instrumental music combined with nature sounds.

   Music is the perfect companion when you need more energy and also when you need to relax. Some well-chosen music can do wonders for your state of mind.

5. **Spend 30–60 minutes of quality time with your spouse.** During this time you can harmonize your states and understand each other's 'journeys' throughout that day. Periodic reconnections maintain the strength of your relationship. Each of us needs to be understood and appreciated by those we care

about. Without these moments of mutual support, the relationship becomes shallow and fragile.

6. **Take 15 minutes to revise your day**. Evaluate what worked and what didn't.

   It's okay to make mistakes out of a desire to progress. But it's not okay to make the same mistakes because you haven't taken the necessary time to learn from the previous times, so that you can avoid making them again in similar contexts. Those who evolve quickly learn more through their own mistakes rather than the mistakes of others.

7. **Make peace with yourself.** It is important to realize that you've done all that you could during the day that's about to end.

   The following affirmation helps me because it allows me to make peace with my past and look confidently towards the future. 'I am in the best possible place to get from here to where I desire.'

8. **Take 5 minutes to clarify your top three priorities for the following day**. Figure out how much time each of them will take and how the results will look.

   Clarity is essential in obtaining excellence. Without clarity, you can only achieve top results by accident. You need to sow before you reap. And the process of planning in the evening holds the best seeds for your success.

9. **Free yourself from any anxieties through writing.** Release those harmful thoughts that are keeping you feeling tense. Don't hold them in; it's best if you let them out through writing, after you have become aware of them.

10. **Call your parents and share with them 1–2 beautiful things** that have happened to you during the day.

    Your family's support is a fundamental element for your personal success. Achievements that are only appreciated by strangers and not your loved ones are not worth much.

11. **Spend at least an hour of quality time with your children** (time during which you are not interrupted by outside stimuli) and reconnect with what's truly important in your life. Children grow up so fast, the time that passes cannot be taken back...and any regrets you might have afterwards will be too late.

12. **Become aware of how you nourished your values today.** Did you do what was important to you...or to others? Do you need to make some adjustments tomorrow? And if you do, then do them, because time goes by so quickly and you have the right to live the best life you possibly can!

13. **Eat a light meal alongside those dearest to you.** Chew slowly to ease your digestion. The more you chew, the less your stomach will take to digest the

food and the more restful your sleep will be.

14. **Take a warm shower** that cleanses your body but also your mind and your emotions.

   For many people, me included, water has a special energizing and balancing effect. I'm aware that this is not the case for everyone, but if you feel the same, take advantage of this method to harmonize your body, mind and emotions.

15. **Remember the things you're grateful for as soon as your head hits the pillow**. The studies I've read, as well as my own experience, have shown me that there's a powerful link between the type of energy you have before you sleep and the type of energy you have when you wake up. A smooth glide towards sleep, from a place of feeling grateful, will facilitate a pleasant and restful sleep.

In contrast, revisiting all of the problems you had during the day, before falling asleep, will result in a restless and unpleasant sleep. So carefully choose the type of energy you have before going to bed.

Now that you have a lot more ideas about how you can end your weekdays a lot better, you'll be able to organize your evening so that the following day will be a remarkable one!

So, prepare your sleep carefully, so that in the morning, you'll be energized, focused, confident and full of purpose!